BAD

LP LOVELL STEVIE J. COLE

BAD

Published in the United States of America.

Cover Model: Rick Van Den Bosch
Photographer: Eric Max Ellis
Cover Design: Max Elis

You can also follow the BAD playlist on Stevie J. Cole's Spotify!

Prologue

Ronan

"Simple Man"- Deftones

The fireplace crackles before a log collapses, sending tiny embers flitting up the chimney. My father stares at me from across the room. The heat from the fire caressing my skin, and I fight a smile as I stare back at the anger swimming in his eyes.

"You did *what*?" he says through clenched teeth.

"I made a deal with the Americans." I shove my hands in my pocket, carefully wrapping my fingers around the knife I made sure to tuck deep inside.

He swats his hand over his face, his cheeks reddening. His nostrils flare. "You made a business deal behind my back? And with the Americans?" There's such a small amount of restraint in his voice, and I find a sick amusement in it.

"It makes complete sense," I say. "They have no gunrunning laws. It gives us a foothold into Mexico." I smile. "The cartels would pay well."

He shakes his head, his jaw ticking. My father is so very set in the old ways of the Bratva. Honor. Dignity, and while I can respect that, my father is a hypocrite. I learned early in life that honor and dignity do nothing but limit your power.

"I do not make deals with Americans. The *Bratva* does not make deals with the Americans!"

"I will run the Bratva when you die, and—"

"You're only eighteen!" He pushes up from his chair and steps toward me. He wants to hit me, I know it, but these days I'm much bigger than he is. He knows he can no longer beat me into submission. His jaw tenses when he comes face to face with me, seething. "You are too power hungry, Ronan."

"No, you are too weak." My fingers curl around the hilt of the knife, and I wait for my heart to race or skip, but it never does. Given the amount of times I've thought about this, the time it took to plan, I had hoped this would feel more momentous, but I feel nothing. And with that thought, I pull my hand from my pocket and slice the blade across his neck, around his jaw from ear to ear.

His eyes widen as he clutches at his throat, gasping and gurgling for a breath he'll never catch.

"A smart man sees what he wants and takes it," I say with a smug smile, watching the blood stream over his knuckles like a beautiful, ruby waterfall. Part of me wants to bathe in it, for this is my baptism. The moment of my true birth, the day I'll look back on as the moment I first took power into my hands. My father staggers back into the wall before slumping to the floor.

"It's only business," I say. "I do hope you understand, you would have only stood in my way." With that, I turn around, tossing the knife into the fireplace. Igor and Boris step out from the shadow of the kitchen, and I nod toward my father's body. "Get rid of it."

"Yes, boss," they say in unison.

I walk out of the room the new leader of the Russian Bratva, but I promise, that's not where I'll stop. Some may think what I just did was callous, and I'd agree. It was. So very cruel, but true power is never held by good men.

Chapter 1

Ronan

12 years later

"I Don't Care" - Apocylptica, Adam Gontier

The celloist in the corner of the ballroom plays a drab tune. Women in lavish gowns flit around the room while the men in tuxedos watch their every move. To be honest, I hate the formalities of political campaigns. It's all a show, after all, a power play. Ironically, none of the people in this room *truly* hold power. For a man in control must be the most perfect of villains, and heartless power is the only absolute authority there is.

Prime Minister Vasily steps to the side of the room, and I spot Anastasia clinging to Nikoli Derevichi's arm. Wisps of blonde hair frame her elegant face. Her dress fits just so. My, she is the epitome of a refined woman...at least on paper. She glances at me, a light blush painting her pale cheeks before Nikoli leans down to whisper something in her ear. He steps to the side with a group of men. I turn away, sipping the bland Chardonnay because I know Ana will be making her way over here at any moment. She is so very predictable. *How mundane.*

Within seconds, a delicate hand brushes my shoulder. "Ronan?" Anastasia whispers. Her fingers trail along my arm as she steps into my line of vision. "Where have you been?"

"You shouldn't touch me in public, Ana." I lift the glass of wine to my lips, nodding across the room toward Nikoli, her husband *and* the President of Russia. I force my brow to wrinkle as though I'm concerned with him. *Lies.* He should be concerned with me.

"I need you, Ronan." Her eyes drag over my body. "I crave you."

I inhale, pretending I'm torn. "Ah, Anastasia... Careful." Nikoli's gaze cuts over toward us. A slight smirk plays at my lips as our eyes lock from across the room—two men battling for the affection of one woman. *So suspenseful.*

"Ronan..." Anastasia whines.

Desperation is such an unattractive quality to possess. It's not that I want Anastasia, but that I *need* her. Every step I take is planned, calculated, and Anastasia is simply a piece to the puzzle I've spent the last seven years constructing. So, I smile and bite down on my lip as though I'm restraining myself from taking her into the hallway and fucking her. "Not here," I whisper before I step away, heading toward the patio.

The frigid air and a flurry of snow greet me when I open the door. I pause in the doorway to pull the cigar from my breast pocket and light it. Smoke swirls in front of my face as I stare at the lights of Moscow dotting the horizon. I wonder what it will feel like when all of this is mine? Smiling at the thought, I turn to watch through the window as all the little puppets dance on strings they don't know they're tied to.

My jaw clenches when I spot Ivan Menova speaking with Nikoli. My pulse throbs. When Ivan notices me watching him, an uneasy smile shapes his lips. He shakes Nikoli's hand, combing his fingers through his hair as he heads to the doorway. As soon as Ivan steps foot onto the snow, he shivers. "It's cold tonight," he says.

I take a slow drag of my cigar, the bright red glow of the cherry casting shadows over his face. I don't say a word. I can see the worry setting in on his furrowed brow. Fear is like blood in the water, it beckons me. It sends a jolt of adrenaline through me, sparking a want for violence.

"Another shipment goes out to Pakistan this Friday," he says.

Laughing, I blow smoke directly in his face and he coughs. This man has the audacity to approach me? I know he's had men intercepting shipments of my ammunition to the Middle East. And I'm not certain whether he's brave or just stupid, which is why I've not had him killed. *Yet.*

Stupidity warrants a humane form of death, but bravery—tsk, tsk.

"Mr. Cole," he says. "The shipment."

"Tell me, Ivan. Do you take me for a stupid man?"

"No, of course not." There's a slight tremor to his voice. *Poor soul.*

I hand my cigar to Ivan, and his forehead wrinkles with confusion before his cheeks wash white. He stammers over unintelligible words. Stupidity does get people into such trouble sometimes...I take a single step toward him and place my lips so close by his ear that I can feel the heat from his skin, smell the cheap aftershave he's doused himself in. "I know what you've done, Ivan. Enjoy that cigar, it will be your last."

He drops the cigar and when he turns to run, Igor is already blocking his way. Clasping my hands together, I step to the side. There's only a small pop of air from the silencer when the trigger is pulled, and Ivan falls face first into the pile of snow at the doorway. I smile because the splattering of blood does look quite festive.

I straighten my suit, and step over the body, walking back into the warmth of the party. After all, it would look suspicious if I left so suddenly, wouldn't it? I may hate the niceties of these political campaigns, but I do so enjoy the business dealings sometimes involved. Several people stop me to talk and I oblige, eventually excusing myself. I grab a glass of wine and lean against the far wall, waiting.

The quartet plays on and then a man yells. I glance up just as he runs in from the patio, and my body tingles with anticipation. “A man’s been shot!” he shouts. Women shriek, men scurry around with cell phones to their ears. There's quite the commotion forming over Ivan lying in a puddle of blood, and I simply stand here, utterly amused by them all. Death is a natural part of life. I don't understand why everyone gets so upset. My observation is interrupted by the vibration of my phone in my trouser pocket. I fish it out and place it to my ear. "Yes?"

"Jésus did not accept the offer," Boris says.

My jaw twitches and my pulse tick, tick, ticks up, thrumming in my throat. "I'm sorry. *What* did you say, Boris?"

"He won't sell the land."

I stare across the room at Anastasia as she clings to her pathetic husband's arm. "Get me a flight to Mexico. Now," I say before I hang up, shove the phone in my pocket, and walk out of the party with my fists clenched at my sides.

I have business to tend to.

The next morning, I sit in front of Jésus Garcia's desk with Igor and Boris beside me. I check my watch before staring through the window at the barren landscape. The desert hills of Juarez seem to stretch on for an eternity, hot and scorched.

I've decided I hate Mexico. I hate the cartels, the lack

of finesse and respect they possess. They're nothing more than savages with ammunition, but unfortunately for me, the Sinaloa cartel own land I am very much in need of. Maybe when I'm done with it, I'll blow their entire city of Juarez clean off the map. *Maybe...*

The door to the office creaks open and Jésus walks in dressed in a cheap suit. Several men toting guns follow him into the room. *The cartels and their guns...* Jésus' ink black hair is slicked back, and there's a permanent crease in his forehead. His eyes set on me as he steps behind his desk and takes a seat. "I don't make deals with Russians." He smiles, and I fully expect for a gold tooth to glint in the light, but it doesn't. *How very disappointing.*

"Four million dollars," I say, adjusting my cufflinks. "I will give you four million dollars for the land surrounding Lago Estrellado."

"No." He plucks a half-smoked cigar from the ashtray on his desk and lights it.

I stare at him, one side of my lips ticking up in an annoyed smile. "I don't think you understand the generosity I'm providing you with this offer."

"I shit on your generosity." Jésus grins wide. "As I said, I don't make deals with Russians."

My pulse drums in my neck, blood rushes to my face. "I'll assume you don't understand who you are dealing with, and I will give you one more opportunity to make a wise decision, my friend."

"I know who you are, and I don't give a shit!"

Closing my eyes, I draw in a breath. I don't accept no. Ever. I open my eyes and push up from my seat, giving Jésus a passing glance as I head toward the door of his office. *I tried to be nice, I did.*

Now, what to do about him? Murder is so boring, and if Jésus is killed without strategic planning, another leader will just step into his place. I'm one for the theatrics, the festivities, so I'll simply play a little game of chess. Pit cartel against cartel, sit back and watch the carnage like an emperor at a gladiator show. And then, when Rome lies in ruins, I'll swoop in and take my land. For free.

Once we're in the car, I glance at Igor. "Find out everything you can about the Juarez cartel and Gabriel Estrada, would you, Igor? Nothing like having Jésus taken down by his own enemy."

Chapter 2

Camilla

6 months later

"Whore" – In This Moment

Jésus stands in the middle of the foyer surrounded by heavily armed men, and I stand in the hallway, watching. He crooks a finger to motion me over. I force a smile as I make my way into the room, and stop in front of him. "My love," he says, "I must go kill your brother and all his little friends." He strokes my cheek, and I fight the wave of revulsion threatening to rise.

"Ah, Jésus, I do hope he kills you," I say.

His face reddens, and his jaw tenses before he heads toward the door followed by half an army. Once the door closes, I turn and walk through the house, thinking about how weak Jésus is.

Wars are fought all the time. Men die for causes that are not their own: power, money, even love. But no wars are bloodier than those of the cartels. The money and power is absolute and unrivaled. Men will fight and die for such things, and Jésus is no different. The ironic thing is: I am supposed to be his collateral, the sister he kidnapped to keep Gabriel, his enemy, in line. He doesn't realize the real enemy is the one sleeping in his bed, listening to every tidbit of information. Spotting every weakness. The fact that he's gone to fight my brother instead of killing me shows just how far he's fallen into my trap.

Yes, Jésus is weak, and it *will* get him killed.

As I wander the near empty house, I imagine how pretty the villa would look engulfed in flames; Jésus' men screaming in agony as their skin melts from their bodies. The thought brings a smile to my face, but, alas, I must bide my time. If my brother fails to kill Jésus, I'll have to do it, and it's so much easier to slit a man's throat while he's fucking you than when he has a gun pointed at your head.

I pass the pool table in the game room, trailing my fingers over the felt on my way to the bar in the corner. I pour a glass of brandy and take a sip. The alcohol burns on its way down, and I close my eyes, picturing all the ways Gabriel might kill Jésus. It will be bloody and gruesome, of course. A death fit for a boss— a message.

There's a loud bang and the ground rocks, startling me. Bits of plaster crumble away from the ceiling as the chandelier above my head swings precariously. *What the fuck?* I hurry to the window. Men in black military gear rush into the courtyard. This is not Jésus, and it's not Gabe. I have to assume whoever this is, is an enemy. And as far as anyone is concerned, I'm Jésus' whore which means I'm as good as dead if they find me. The rapid *pop, pop, pop* of gunfire rings out, and I immediately drop to a crouch and press my back to the wall. *Shit.*

I crawl to the pool table and feel around beneath it. *Surely these fucktards have a gun strapped under here somewhere? Nothing. Damn it!* Footsteps pound down the hallway, and I grab a pool cue, snapping it over my knee. I clutch the splintered pieces of wood in each hand as I rush to the door, pressing my back to the wall. The handle lowers and the door opens before a dust covered boot steps over the threshold.

Dropping to one knee, I slam the jagged wood into the man's thigh before he even makes it inside. He screams in pain, hitting the floor with a thud. I raise the other piece of broken wood high and aim for the skin at the base of his neck, but freeze when cool metal touches the back of my head. *The barrel of a gun.* I may be angry and unhinged, but I'm not an idiot.

"Hands behind your back." His thick Russian accent makes me bristle.

I slowly place my hands behind me. He ties them together with a cable, then uses them to force me through the house toward Jésus' office. Of course I could fight. I could attempt to run, but I don't. I prefer to know who I'm fighting, or what I'm running from. The man drags me inside the office and forces me into a chair with my hands still behind my back.

"You stupid fucks." I laugh. "Do you know whose house this is? You will all die." I hate Jésus, but right now I hope he kills these Russian bastards.

The man pulls a cloth from his pocket and crams it inside my mouth, then ties another piece of material around my head to hold the gag in place. He pats the top of my head before he leaves. And here I sit bound and gagged, listening to an all-out war ensue.

It's several minutes before the door creaks open again, but the man who walks inside this time... well, he's not like any soldier I've ever seen. His three-piece suit clings perfectly to his muscular frame. His dark hair swoops up neatly, screaming of sex and money, and his sapphire eyes hone in on me the way I imagine a shark hones in on its helpless prey right before it strikes. Some men command power while others simply *are* power. This man wears it like a second skin, an impenetrable suit of armor. I've seen bad men, but this one...he's *really* bad. And I know instantly that I'm fucked.

He stops in front of me without a word, brushing his finger over my cheek as he reaches around to untie my gag. As soon as the gag is free, I spit at him. "Vete a la verga culero!"

A laugh rumbles up his throat. "I do love a feisty woman."

With a deft flick of his wrist he unfastens the buttons of his jacket and rounds the desk to take a seat. Leaning back in the chair, he pulls a small tin from his suit pocket and opens it, producing a cigar. He rolls the cigar between his fingers, his eyes fixing on me as though I'm something fascinating—a new toy maybe.

I watch his lips wrap around the cigar as he tilts his head, and flips a lighter open. The flame sparks to life, dancing over the end until it glows a bright, cherry red. It's such a simple act and yet he makes it look like art, a masterclass in elegant masculinity.

"Why so angry, Krasivaya?" he asks, smoke slipping through his lips.

My blood heats. "You will die Russian."

"Hmm, I doubt that. Jésus will be dead by now." He takes another puff from the cigar. "Tell me, what is your name?"

"What's yours?"

"Ronan Cole." He grins.

Oh. Fuck. I am so ridiculously screwed. He's not just a Russian, he's *the* Russian. A Bratva kingpin that even the strongest of cartels have a healthy respect for. What the hell is *he* doing in Mexico? I'm never caught off-guard, but right now, I don't know what to do or say because the stories about this guy... He's more myth than reality. I narrow my eyes, vaguely recalling a conversation Jésus had with his second in charge bragging about how he'd refused to sell some land to the Russian. *This Russian?* God, Jésus never was the smartest.

Ronan's eyes spark and I study him. He's so young, maybe thirty. I expected *the* Ronan Cole to look just like the cliché bad guy in every mobster film: old and creepy, but...

"Now, what is *your* name?" he asks.

"Camilla," I say quietly.

A small smirk touches his lips, and he taps the ash off his cigar into an ashtray. "Camila *Estrada*?" His accent caresses my name and awareness crackles up my spine.

"Yes."

"Well, well, isn't this an interesting turn about? I was unaware that you were sleeping with the enemy." He laughs. "Your brother will be so very disappointed."

"Fuck you!"

Ronan's gaze falls to my chest before leisurely gliding over my body. "Gladly," he says, his voice dropping an octave as though to fuck the word. I shift in my seat. "I can see why you would make the perfect ventana," he says. "You would be an awful weakness to any man." He props his elbow on the desk and inhales another, long drag from his cigar. "Donovan!" he shouts, his gaze never straying from mine. The door opens and footsteps cross the floor behind me. "Take her." Ronan smiles. "Put her in the car."

The large man steps forward and unties me before hauling me to my feet. *Fuck no, I am not going with him!* I fight against his hold, twisting around to rake the nails of my free hand down his cheek. He grunts and growls, but never loosens his hold. Suddenly, Ronan moves in front of me and grabs my jaw. He pulls me toward him, pressing his hard body against mine. His domineering presence forces me into a submission I didn't know I possessed.

"Keep fighting, little kitty. I will only break you," he says on a low growl, his breath washing over my face.

"Vieta a la meierda." I say, spitting at him.

I'm dragged from the room with Ronan Cole smiling like a devil incarnate.

Chapter 3

Ronan

"My Way"- Chase Holfelder

The sweltering sun causes sweat to prickle across my brow. Gnats and mosquitoes swarm around me, and I swat them away as I wade through the tall, dried weeds. "This is absolutely deplorable," I mumble.

The grass eventually thins out and nothing but sand surrounds the crystal blue lake. "Ah," I say, spreading my arms wide as I throw my head back on a laugh. "How glorious." I take in a deep breath. The scent of desert sand is like pure gold, because what lies underneath that lake... "How long do you think it will take to drain?" I ask, facing Igor.

"Four days." Igor swipes at the bugs buzzing around his face.

"Perfect." I stare across the smooth water more than pleased with how things have turned out. I've acquired this land for free and now have an entire cartel under my thumb.

And really, what better way to transport the mineral I'll be mining from this very spot than through the masters of illusive export: the cartel? Sometimes I can't help but think fate is on my side. I really can't.

When I turn and head toward the plane at the end of the field, I catch sight of Donovan dragging a very angry Camilla from the car. She's spitting and cursing, her face red as she strains against his hold. He leans toward her and she head-butts him. He goes staggering back, dazed and she takes off sprinting across the field.

I glance at Igor and roll my eyes. "Go fetch her," I say, pulling a handkerchief from my pocket and dabbing the sweat from my brow.

Igor storms after Camilla, his long legs taking strides twice the length of hers. He catches her by the hair, yanking her to the ground. Oh, she's screaming and swatting at Igor as he drags her toward the waiting plane, and I do find it rather entertaining. *Such a feisty little thing*.

The engines to the plane cut on, the propellers whirring to life and kicking up dust as I leisurely make my way toward Igor and Camilla. "Turn her around," I say.

Camilla's eyes flare with defiance before Igor grabs her and spins her around. On a sigh, I step behind her, wrap my arm around her throat, and lean over her shoulder, nestling my face to her cheek. I drag in the scent of hibiscus that hangs heavy in her hair before I press my forearm harder against her throat. "You will learn," I whisper and kiss her jaw.

She claws and fights me as I increase the pressure over her windpipe, but only for a second, because she soon goes completely limp. Igor grabs her when I release her. "Sedate her, then gag her." I glance at Igor. "I can't be bothered to listen to her nonsense when she wakes up."

Chapter 4

Camilla

"Power" - Kanye West

I'm jostled awake by a bump and pounding headache. My pulse races, and a loud screeching noise pierces my ears. *Where the fuck am I?* There's another bump. I glance around. I'm in the cabin of a plane. *Great! He drugged me and shoved me on a plane.*

Ronan sits across from me, studying his phone. Anger ripples through my veins as I stare at him. The plane slows to a stop, and I yank at the seatbelt. Ronan glances up from his phone, snapping his fingers. Igor appears from nowhere and grabs onto my arm, dragging me from my seat.

"Welcome to Russia," Ronan says with a condescending smile.

Dirty Russian bastard. My blood simmers through my veins. I've been in this situation before and anger will do nothing to help me. I need a clear head. A plan. He stands, adjusting his suit jacket as he walks toward me. His eyes narrow and he reaches for my neck, his warm fingertips skirting over my throat. "Bruises suit you," he says. I want to slap him.

The door to the plane opens, revealing a flurry of snow and ice. Ronan ducks through the door and trudges down the steps and across the icy tarmac. I grit my teeth, glaring at his back as he disappears inside a black SUV. Igor shoves me through the opening and down the stairs, my cheeks stinging from the cold as he directs me toward the car. He yanks open the door, shoves me inside next to Ronan, then closes the door, silencing the raging wind outside.

The car pulls away and his eyes lock on me, void of all emotion. The hairs on the back of my neck stand on end. For the first time in my life, I feel like prey. A lamb with its back to a lion, and the thought has me clenching my jaw.

"What do you want with me?" I ask, unable to contain the frustration any longer.

"I'm not sure yet." He grins like a bastard in his pristine suit, smoking his fancy cigar. He has to have a reason.

"You're not sure." I narrow my eyes. "So, what? You just took me on a whim?"

"How do I put it? You were a rather *lovely* surprise."

"Let me guess, you thought you'd stick it to Jésus, steal his whore?" I roll my eyes. "You do realize whores are a dime a dozen."

He tosses his head back on a deep laugh, smoke

billowing from his lips. "Come now, you're Gabriel Estrada's sister. So tell me, Camilla, were you really Jésus Garcia's helpless whore?" An arrogant smile shapes his lips. "I don't think so."

He can't know... "I was Jésus' captive, taken to keep my brother from waging war. You can't blame a girl for making life a little easier on herself."

"That is what you would have people believe." His eyes spark with amusement. "But I know better."

Fuck, fuck, fuck! How can he possibly know that?

"I know everything about you." He leans across the seat. "You are powerless now. Helpless..."

Anger flashes through me hot and fast, and my nails bite into my palms leaving a sharp sting behind. What could he possibly want me for? I force myself to look away, picturing all the ways I want to kill this Russian fuck in an attempt to collect myself.

We wind through endless miles of snow-covered woods before the car slows, coming to a stop outside an ornate golden gate. The driver rolls the window down and spits something in Russian to the guard standing outside. Laughing, the guard steps back, presses a button, and the motor to the gate whirs to life. The car takes a slight turn and a large, white mansion comes into view. Beside it sits another building. Men with rifles strapped to their backs pass in and out of the doorway, and in front of the building are rows of SUVs with guns mounted to the hoods. *Jesus, does he have his own personal army or something?*

We come to a stop in front of the main house, and Ronan exhales as though he's put out. The driver practically runs around to the side of the car, tripping over himself to open Ronan's door. Ronan climbs out without a word or even a glance in my direction. I watch him walk up the marble stairs, his perfectly tailored suit clinging to his large frame. He snaps his fingers and my door opens. The sudden cold that rushes in from outside causes my breath to catch in my throat.

Igor reaches inside and grabs my elbow, pulling me from the car as he mumbles something in Russian. I'm lead up the stairs to the wooden doorway, and the massive door creaks open. Ronan steps inside, releasing an exasperated breath, and I'm shoved in after him.

The gold and crystal chandeliers hanging from the cathedral ceilings cast a warm glow over the winding stairwell. Renaissance art hangs on every wall. Thick oriental rugs cover the marble. It looks like somebody vomited old money all over the place. Ronan disappears down a hallway as I'm lead to a room on the upper level.

Igor throws the door open and shoves me inside. "Dinner is at nine," he says. "There's a dress on the bed. Mr. Cole requests that you wear it." And then, he leaves, closing the door behind him and locking it.

My heart bangs in my chest as I look around the room. Another offensive oriental rug sits beneath a four-poster bed, and there, on the thick bedspread is a black dress bag which I look at with disdain. Men are so predictable in that they think I'm predictable — a pretty girl. Nothing but the innocent sister of a cartel boss. I smile. This man will be no different, so I'll play his doll long enough to work out what he wants at least. After all, you can't beat a man without knowing his weaknesses. I may be well and truly outgunned, but I am not without my own weapons.

He's right. I set Jésus up. He thought he took me as a captive, but I was there willingly, getting close to the enemy. Lying in wait. The Russian may have taken me, but he will not find me an easy captive.

Chapter 5

Ronan

"Filthy Pride"- Social Response

The butler pours two glasses of merlot before leaving the room. I raise the glass below my nose, breathing in the hearty tannins just as Igor steps inside the room, dragging a very angry Camilla behind him. My gaze follows her feminine curves. "I see the dress fits you very nicely," I smirk into my glass while Igor shoves Camilla into a chair.

She shoots daggers at me and snatches her arm away from Igor. I study her as she subtly glances around the room, and her eyes lock on the large, stained glass window behind the table. There's a slight flicker in her turquoise eyes, as though she thinks she may possibly escape. I'll let her think what she wants for now. At the very least, it should be entertaining.

"So," her gaze slowly drifts to me, "you like to dress women like dolls?" The words roll from her tongue, and I won't lie, her accent is quite alluring. "I had no idea you and

Jésus have so much in common," she says before lifting her glass to her lips.

"You wound me, Krasivaya," I say, placing my hand over my heart. "He and I have nothing in common."

"Enough of the shit. What do you want, Russian?"

"Such language," I tsk before placing my glass on the table. *Do I tell her that I know who she really is? No, I think I'll save that.* "You're collateral."

"Collateral for what? Jésus?"

I smile. "You ask too many questions."

"Oh, I'm sorry. I'd like to know why you've dragged me to this hell hole, how rude of me." She rolls her eyes.

I release an exasperated sigh. "Your brother's cooperation is needed for a short time."

"Is that so? What could a Russian possibly want with my brother?"

"It's of no concern to you."

"Maybe you just wanted a new whore?" She tilts her head and a wave of ebony hair pours over her shoulder. "You're such a *charming* individual, I can't see *why* you'd have to force a girl."

My jaw ticks from her insult. "Do they raise everyone in Mexico without the slightest hint of respect?"

"I'm Colombian. I was raised to respect few things. Power. Money. And *blood*." She taps one nail over the stem of her wine glass. "The kind that would stain that designer suit of yours."

"How *very* dramatic."

The butler steps back into the room, placing our plates in front of us before exiting again. A small plume of steam rises from the filet mignon. I open my linen napkin, laying it delicately across my lap before taking my fork and knife in hand. Just as I cut into the steak, something whistles past my ear followed by a muted thud behind me. I look up slowly to find Camilla standing with her palms flat on the table, glaring at me like an angry jungle cat. "Shit," she says with a growl.

I glance over my shoulder. There's a steak knife now embedded in the wall. *How savage.* I knew she was volatile, but, I'll admit, I may have underestimated her. Most people fear me like death itself. However, Camilla does not fear me, and I'd be lying if I said the idea of teaching her to doesn't utterly excite me.

On a sigh, I drop my fork to my plate and scoot my chair back. When I stand, I see her brace against the table, her eyes boring into me as I approach. She arches a single brow in a dare, and I do so like a dare... I grab her by the throat, digging my fingers into her jawline as I lift her up. Dishes and glasses break when I throw her to the table and pin her down by the neck. Most women would scream and claw at my hand, but I barely feel her pulse pick up.

Shoving my knee between her thighs, I force them apart and step between them. With a smile, I lean over her and place my lips right by her ear. The sweet scent of her skin makes every bit of man in me bristle with tension. "It would not be wise to test me," I whisper against her warm throat.

Her leg wraps around my waist without warning, the heel of her shoe digging into me when she pulls me against her. My grip on her throat tightens while she fights to lift her neck from the table. I allow her an inch, and she places her lips at the shell of my ear. Her heated breath fans across my skin like a fire, and my fingers twitch over her throat. Camilla is the type of woman any man would love to fuck, and I'm certain she's reduced many men of power to blubbering messes by techniques such as this, but it takes more than beauty and curves to sway me.

"I've tested men far worse than you," she says.

"There are no worse men than me," I whisper.

I keep waiting for her heartbeat to quicken beneath my fingertips, for the fear to set in, but her pulse remains steady. And when I tighten my hold again, she groans. I close my eyes and swallow. Survival instincts tend to be engrained deep, but this woman's absence of fear nearly makes me drunk with excitement. I open my eyes and grab a knife from the table, immediately dragging the blade along the inside of her thigh, waiting. Waiting for her pulse to beat fast and hard, and while it does pound faster, this is not the pace of fear. This is want. Basic lust. This is the dark side of humanity calling to be tamed. I drag the blade higher and higher until my knuckles brush the lace of her underwear.

Her legs fall shamelessly open. Now this, *this* is dangerous because it beckons my depravity in a way I've never experienced. Fear is one thing...this is much more intoxicating, because I can almost imagine cutting her while I fuck her. My dick swells, and I drop my chin to my chest fighting to maintain myself.

"I *will* kill you, Russian," she says before her teeth rake the side of my throat. I can't help but fight a groan at her sweet promise.

"And I will hurt you, Krasivaya..." I pull back and nip at her bottom lip before skirting my tongue along its curve. I'm so tempted to bite harder and draw blood. "In ways you can't possibly imagine," I whisper.

"Promises, promises." She smiles against my mouth.

"Well, I do always make good on my promises." I press the blade into her thigh, piercing her skin as I slowly drag it over her leg. She gasps and bites her lip on a moan. *Oh, dear god...* A trickle of warm blood rolls over my knuckles, and I have to close my eyes to control myself because if I see that blood... Inhaling, I shove against her and push away from the table with the knife still clutched in my hand.

I snap my fingers as I walk out of the room, and two men immediately brush past me. I hear her swear at them. Dishes break. My cock strains against my pants as I storm down the hallway to the living room and slam the door closed behind me. I assumed she would be a challenge, but I never believed she would be without fear. She is worthy prey, for what greater thrill is there than that of the hunt? The kill is merely a result.

I glance down at the knife. The specks of blood on the blade cause my pulse to hammer in my chest. My mind jumbles with thoughts of her lips, of how volatile it would be to fuck her, cut her…I pace the room, dragging my hand down my face.

She is one, I know, will be so beautiful when she bleeds.

Chapter 6

Ronan

"Shameless"- Massive Metal Covers

"The Bank of China is scheduled to call at noon," Olga says, reading over a printout of today's calendar. "After that, the British National; the branch in Prague will be sending reports over at one. And at four Mr. Voytanoksy is scheduled to go over the international departments."

Closing my eyes, I take a breath. I don't really want to be bothered with this nonsense, but this is how I blend in with society—under the ruse of an accomplished businessman. After all, every criminal needs their front, and the World Bank is mine.

"Thank you, Olga." I take the report from her and step inside my office. The door barely shuts before I pull my phone from my pocket. I dial a number in Mexico; the foreign ringtone beeps as I walk to the blinds and peek through. It's terribly sad how the people outside run about only to make ends meet. *Would be such a pity to be poor.*

Powerless...

The line clicks. "You have my sister, you Russian fuck!" Gabriel shouts over the phone before I hear him spit.

"Such a temper," I tut as I take a seat behind my desk. "Must run in the family."

"Fuck you and your pale ass!"

"Is that any way to talk to the man you're a slave to?" I smile even though he can't see me. "Yes, I have your dear Mila—isn't that what you call her? So, I assume you'll do whatever I ask to ensure her safety?"

He remains silent, because while Gabriel Estrada may be ruthless, he is not heartless. Threaten a man and you force his loyalty for merely a second, *buy* a man, and he'll forever be indebted to you. And this is where I pat myself on the back because what better way to purchase a man's soul than through his very heart?

"You do wish her to remain alive?" I ask, and again I'm met by silence. I can only imagine his face is red with anger. "Marvelous!" I say.

"I want to talk to her."

"Understandable. I'll have her call you and fill you in on what a wonderful time she's having when I get home."

"Fuck you!"

There's no point in meaningless insults, so I get to business. "There will be a shipment of guns coming into Juarez, you'll make sure they make it across the American border."

There's a long pause. I hear him swallow. I face the computer screen, tapping my fingers over my keyboard as I pull up the cameras to Camilla's room. She's pacing like a caged lioness, roughly dragging her hands through her hair.

"Come, come, Gabriel, I'd hate to let my men have their way with your sister. And might I add, she has a very tempting figure."

A string of profanities come across the line. "Do not hurt her, you—"

"So... we have an agreement?"

He sighs, defeat lacing that sound. "Yes."

"Very well. Pleasure doing business with you and your family, Estrada." I disconnect the call and stare at the screen, watching Camilla. I can only imagine she's swearing in Spanish.

The office phone buzzes and I close the browser before I press the button. "Yes?"

"Ms. Derevechi is here."

"Ah, yes, to go over President Derevichi's account. Fantastic," I say with a grin. "Send her in." I stand from my chair and cross the room, ensuring the blinds are open just enough for the photographer across the street to get a good shot. After all, I'm paying him good money, and I wouldn't want to waste it...

The secretary escorts Anastasia in, and my, she is every bit the President's wife in that knee-length, emerald dress. "Let me know if I can get you anything," Olga says before closing the door behind her.

Sexual frustration brims off Ana. Lust. I bite my lip and stare at her like I want nothing more in this life than to make her come. She takes a step toward me, and I grab her long hair, fisting it and yanking her head back. I pin her body between me and the wall as I trail my nose along the curve of her neck. "Is this what you want?" I ask, grabbing the hem of her dress and hitching it up her thighs.

She claws at my suit jacket. "Yes," she whispers.

Every breath I take is planned and measured, and this is no different. Nikoli Derevichi will know I've had his wife, and I can only hope he'll threaten me.

Chapter 7

Camilla

"Run for Cover" – The Killers

The man with the scarred face smiles at me when I'm shoved into the chair. My eyes focus on the laptop on the table. Pain ricochets through every inch of my body. Everything around me sounds muted. My wrists are pulled behind me and cable tied to the chair.

A window pops up on the laptop screen, and my papa's face comes into view.

"Ah, Emanuel Estrada," the man with the scarred face says, smiling at my father. "I've had your pretty little daughter for three days now. Are you ready to trade yourself for her yet?" My papa's jaw clenches as he looks at me. I duck my head, unable to look at him. "I have had such fun with her." He strokes my face and bile rises in my stomach. "So sweet. So virginal. She bled all over my cock." He laughs.

"You want me to offer myself so what?" Papa says.

"You can kill me and take my business?"

The man sighs. "Yes."

I fight back tears under the wave of shame that washes over me because my papa knows. He knows that I'm dirty. "Mila." I slowly lift my gaze to the laptop, and Papa looks back at me. "We don't negotiate. You know this."

I squeeze my eyes shut and nod. "I know, Papa." The first rule of business; we do not negotiate, no matter what. Weakness gives our enemies power.

"Stay strong, baby girl. Make me proud." The screen goes black, and I break down into tears.

The man growls and launches the laptop across the room before grabbing my face. "Ah, sweetheart, you and I will have such fun. By the time I send your body back to your daddy, he'll know that you died slowly." He brushes his lips over my cheek. "Painfully."

He moves to the fireplace on the far side of the room, and I whimper because I know what's coming. One of the men in the room cuts the cable ties loose, and I'm thrown to the floor. The material of my shirt is torn from me. The bandages covering my back are peeled away, pulling at my burned skin. I bite down on my lip, fighting the urge to scream.

The scarred man straddles my back, his weight making it hard for me to breathe. A sick laugh slips from his lips. "I do so love desecrating your perfect skin." The red-hot poker sears my back, the skin bubbling underneath it. He presses the poker against my skin over and over until the pain is all I feel. I refuse to scream aloud because I want to make my papa proud, but in my head...in my head I scream until my throat bleeds. I scream for the little girl I was only four days ago, now broken and rocking in a small corner of my mind. I scream...

I wake up screaming, my body drenched in sweat. Dragging desperate breaths into my lungs, I climb out of bed and pace the length of the room as I try to purge myself of the weak thoughts. It's this place, the captivity... It's been weeks, I think. Weeks in the same room. Weeks of searching every inch of the place for an escape, but there is none. There's a single window, and doors that lead onto a balcony, but it's a three-story drop. There's a guard patrol every few minutes—not to mention the cameras in the room. I'd never make the fence in time, and if I did somehow make it through all that, the trek through the frigid, Russian forest would surely kill me.

And so, I'm stuck in this room. Imprisoned with my own nightmares.

This is how it starts—holding me. And when this isn't enough for whatever it is he wants, then comes the rape, the pain, the torture. I clench my jaw and close my eyes. *I can survive it, I always do.* Abuse is simply a contrived attempt at gaining power, but power is all in perception. A man may gain the upper hand by raping a woman, *but* he loses that advantage when a woman becomes willing. Men think sex is a weapon and it is, but not one to be wielded by a man. A woman must know where her power lies and use it shamelessly. I will use whatever means necessary to succeed, and I will never lose, even if I have to sacrifice every fragmented, blackened shard of my soul to win.

My father was right; we don't negotiate and we don't lie down. We fight. In any way we can.

The little red dot to the camera blinks, mocking me. I wonder if Ronan's sitting somewhere watching me slowly fray and splinter, witnessing my weakness. I can picture the smug grin on his face, the air of supremacy floating around him, and it makes my blood boil. Taking the dressing table stool, I storm over to the corner of the room and swing it above my head. I let out a growl and smash that stupid camera off the wall. The wires tear away from the sheetrock, and the device now dangles uselessly from its cords. *Fuck Ronan Cole and his fancy jail cell!*

There's a knock at the door and Igor walks in, a frown set on his face. "The boss wants to see you," he says.

"Oh, I *bet* he does." It's fine. Let him be angry.

Igor leads me out of the room and down the stairwell to a set of double doors. He pushes open one door and walks ahead of me. Towering bookshelves crammed with antique books cover the walls. A shiny grand piano sits in the center of the room, the flames from the fireplace reflecting off its pristine surface. And there's Ronan in one of his suits, sitting on a Victorian sofa with one arm resting along the back. Igor walks over to him and bends at the waist, whispering something in his ear. Ronan's gaze drifts to me, and a wry smile tugs at his lips. "I see," he says as Igor straightens. "Just have another camera installed."

Igor shoots an angry look at me before he turns and walks through the door, leaving me alone with Ronan.

"So nice to see you again, Camilla." Ronan pats the spot next to him as his gaze drops to the low neckline of my dress. "Do sit."

I watch him carefully as I cross the room. And when I sit, I sit as far away from him as possible. He slips his hand inside his coat pocket, pulls out a cigar, and lights it, his eyes locked on me. The smoke swirls around his face. The embers catch in his eyes, and I can't help but think he looks like Satan himself.

"You will not coax a reaction from me," he says, "although I do find it rather distasteful that you would destroy such nice accommodations." He takes another puff from his cigar.

My teeth clench so hard my jaw aches. "Why bother keeping me? You have my brother running around like your errand boy, so kill me already. Threats do not evoke fear, Russian, action does."

His eyes go cold, and he leans toward me. "I want control. Power." He studies me before reaching across the sofa and stroking a single finger over my cheek.

"Fear *is* power."

"Fear is powerless unless there is hope."

"And I thought you were heartless. Careful," I glare at him and lift a brow. "You might disappoint me."

"I'm merciless, Krasivaya, there is a difference." He takes another puff. "Enough chit-chat, I've spoken with your brother."

My heart skips a beat, and I grit my teeth. "I can only imagine how thrilled he was to hear your voice."

"I promised him I would not kill you." His lips quirk up.

"Just kill me already. Gabe won't bend over for you, either way."

"But, he already has."

"Bullshit. A Russian will never run Juarez." I spit on the ground.

He glances at the floor with a snarl of disgust. "Not the most refined, are we?"

"My brother hates Russians even more than I do. He'd sooner watch you slit my throat than work for you." I know Gabe. He loves me and I love him, but Papa always instilled in us that the cartel— the business— must come first. We do not negotiate.

"So certain, little kitty." He laughs.

"You're full of shit!"

"I understand. I do." He nods. "It must be so hard for the leader of the Juarez cartel to come to terms that *she* is now in the presence of the man who dethroned her." He taps a finger over his lips.

He knows who I am, what I am. He thinks he can take my cartel from me? *Deep breaths. Deep, deep breaths.* I clench my fists so hard my nails cut into my palms. "I am Camilla Estrada. I will never be dethroned, *Russian*! Enjoy your moment of victory. It will be short lived, I assure you." I force a smile. If Gabe actually sold out my cartel to this Russian fuck, I'm going to kill him myself!

"*Moment* of victory?" Ronan tosses his head back on a laugh before taking another puff from his stupid cigar.

"You manipulated my brother. He's merely a pawn." Gabriel may be the face of the Juarez cartel but I created it and I control it. Always.

"I prefer the term puppet."

"He's an idiot," I huff. "He has no true power."

"Ah, ah, ah." Ronan's blue eyes dance with some sick form of pleasure. "But you and I are the *only* people who know he is powerless. You've allowed everyone in Mexico to believe he is the king, and so they shall bow to him, and in essence, me." He grins. "Why do you think I took *you*, Camilla?" I glare at him, and his smile widens. He reaches up and grabs my jaw, stroking his thumb over my skin. "You're right, your brother is a pawn. You are the queen. I have taken the queen off the board. Game over, Krasivaya."

I blink. If I weren't so angry I'd probably see the genius in it. He's played it to perfection, manipulated and orchestrated every single play until I couldn't even see it coming. Leading people to believe Gabriel was in charge when it was actually me, is the very thing that has fucked me. "Well played," I whisper.

A cloud of smoke puffs through Ronan's lips. "I would like to tell you how very clever it was to play the wounded little fawn instead of the bloodthirsty lion."

"Fine. You have the cartel, so what do you want from *me*?" I'm fast losing patience, and my temper is wrapping around me like a vine.

"Everything." A sadistic smirk sets on his face, his eyes filled with promises of exactly that...everything.

He shifts and his jacket parts, revealing a white dress shirt pulled tightly over his muscular chest. Beneath that refined exterior there's something lethal and feral. I remember how dangerous his hard body felt pressed against mine, the blade digging into my thigh. The threat. The promise. Few men can make such promises, but this one.... I know he'd deliver. It shouldn't be exciting, but it is. I should be so enraged that he's taken what's mine, but I'm not.

Ronan Cole has presented a challenge: a worthy opponent.

This is not Jésus Garcia following me around with his dick out and dancing to whatever tune my manicured nails tap out. Suddenly everything that came before this feels inconsequential and insignificant. If I can win this, I will win it all. My gaze drifts over his savagely beautiful, chiseled features. What fun I could have playing his twisted game of power. My mind wanders through all the wild and dangerous possibilities. "Well, I look forward to you trying to take it," I say. It's a challenge, a threat, a plea. I don't even know anymore, but I'd love nothing more than to go to war with this bastard.

He leans across the sofa, placing his lips next to my neck. "And that everything includes you." Before I can react, he laughs right in my ear and moves back across the sofa. "Call your brother," he says, pulling a phone from his pocket and handing it to me.

"Why?"

"Don't you want to speak to him?"

"Not on your beckoning."

He thrusts the phone into my hand. "It *wasn't* a request."

"You want my brother to run around like your bitch, you call him." I shove the phone against his chest.

An animalistic growl rumbles from his chest. His hand strikes out like a snake, and he grabs my throat in a bruising grip, but I still smile at him. A small voice in the back of my head tells me to tread carefully, but I've always given that voice the middle finger. His grip tightens and I relish in the pain, the challenge in his hold.

"I won't dance for you, Russian."

He releases me and falls back on the sofa with a laugh.

"You will, or your precious cartel will pay the price. I will pull it apart, piece by piece, ending it with your brother's headless corpse."

"You need the cartel," I say through clenched teeth.

"I don't *need* anything. Now call him, let him know you're *safe and well*."

I want to slap that smug grin off his face, but instead I stand from the couch and dial Gabe's number. I could call the Russians bluff, but sometimes you must pick your battles. I don't need to go to war with him over a phone call. Sadly, my pride doesn't agree, so I must swallow it.

The phone rings twice before the line clicks over. "Hola," Gabe says.

"Gabriel." Ronan watches me from the couch, casually smoking his cigar while commanding his little puppets.

"Camilla!"

"Put him on speaker," Ronan says. I scowl at him, and he simply lifts a brow.

"Is that the fucking Russian?" Gabe asks.

"Yeah." I put the phone on speaker. "Want to tell me why you decided to crawl into bed with him?" I can barely suppress my rage. I'm in this situation because my stupid brother got into some shit while I was behind enemy lines trying to kill Jésus and get our city back.

"It's complicated," he groans, "very complicated, but he helped us get Juarez."

"And now I'm in his house as a prisoner," I say with a

snarl.

"Tell that pale fuck he can suck my Colombian dick!"

My brother is rash and can provoke our enemies like no one else, but he does have a certain way with words. I move over to the piano and lean my elbows on the top. "I've been told to call you. I'm assuming as proof of life," I say, and he sighs. "So what, he threatens to kill me and suddenly you're his bitch?"

"Mila—"

"How is the business?" There's a pause. "Gabe?"

Ronan snaps his fingers. "Enough chit chat," he says. I stare at him and lift a brow.

"Tell that shitfuck to kiss my ass," Gabe says. "Jésus is dead and the Los Zetas are after us."

"Jésus is dead?" All the pieces suddenly click together in my mind. I look at Ronan and a slow smile works over his lips. *Oh, now I see.* Help Gabriel win the war, and then put him on a false throne with his sister as collateral to ensure he plays nice. Clever. Ingenious really. Has Gabriel never heard that you shouldn't make deals with the devil? I take the phone off speaker and press it to my ear. "You made a deal with Ronan?" I say.

Ronan glares at me. "Hang up the phone."

"He had me by the balls," Gabe shouts.

Ronan stands, and I back away, rounding the piano to put it between us. "I don't give a fuck," I growl into the phone. "What could he possibly have on you, Gabriel, you stupid fuck?"

"Every-fucking-thing, Mila! He's like the goddamn devil. I think he owns the fucking FBI!"

Ronan must have heard that, because his lips quirk up. "Little kitty, I'm losing patience." He circles around the piano with his cigar in hand, and I mirror his movements.

"Handle the Los Zetas. Gut their fucking whores, kill their wives and children, burn their businesses to the ground. If you lose me my cartel I will hang you by your own fucking intestines, Gabriel!" I hang up and slide the phone across the piano to Ronan.

"How savage," Ronan's eyes flicker as he picks up the phone.

"I'm offended! You hold me captive while making a deal with my fucktard brother. Why didn't you come to me and make a deal?" I fold my arms over my chest.

"You can't even follow simple instructions to hang up a phone. Why on earth would I make a deal with someone like you? Such a temper." Ronan tsks. He puffs his cigar and steps to the side, and I move the opposite way.

"Ah, but anger is effective," I say.

"But it's really not." A condescending grin crosses his face. "After all, look where it's gotten you."

"You got lucky, Russian." I narrow my eyes at him. "We both know it."

"I'll let you believe what you must. I'd assume it's hard for someone such as you to accept defeat."

I lean forward, bracing my elbows on the piano, and his gaze drops to my chest for a second. "It's when backed into a corner that people are at their most dangerous." I glide my finger over the lacquered piano top. "Like animals."

"And it's also when people are cornered that they are trapped. Like animals." He inhales. "Let me make one thing clear, I am not one to test. You do as I say, when I say it."

"You can hold me captive all you like, Russian, but it doesn't mean I'll play the part."

"I don't know that you understand what the word captive actually means." He leans across the piano toward me, his eyes blazing with some sick form of delight.

"You wouldn't be the first man to try and keep me," I say. *And they all paid the price eventually.* When your father is a powerful drug lord, you become very valuable... to everyone but him.

"No, I don't *try* anything. I succeed with all things." He takes a drag from the cigar, allowing wisps of smoke to creep through his perfect lips. "I will keep you for as long as I please."

"Oh, what fun we'll have," I say sarcastically as I back away from the piano and take a seat on the couch. "All the shit around here I could burn." I run my finger over the arm of his velvet sofa.

His eyes study me while he makes his way around the piano and sits beside me. Maybe I should be careful with him, but I like this thrill of anticipation. I like the way my heart beats in my chest, the unpredictability of it all. He could kill me. He could kiss me. *Possibilities, possibilities.*

"I do not need you, Camilla. Jésus kept you to fuck you. I'm keeping you simply for amusement..." He waves his cigar through the air. "For now, at least."

Without warning, he fists my hair and yanks my face to his lap. My scalp burns as I struggle against him. He's too strong for me to fight and easily holds me down, drowning me in the spicy scent of his cologne as he presses my face harder against his crotch. "I warn you, I bite." I bare my teeth.

He thrusts his hips up, his cock swelling against my cheek. "I can smell your pussy from here," he says. "What fun you and I shall have."

My temper wars with the primal want rapidly tearing through me. I hate him, but the sexual tension between us—the promise of violence—it's like a dizzying form of foreplay that I can't help but partake in.

Fucking asshole. "Didn't take you for a rapist."

He jerks my head to the side, forcing me to look at him. One brow subtly lifts, and suddenly he looks like a dark angel, beautiful and cold. "Now, we *know* that wouldn't be rape. Would it?"

"Fuck you," I spit. "I'd rather fuck a rotting corpse."

He shoves my head away from his lap and stands, glaring down at me. "I expected you to have much stronger survival instincts than this."

"Aw, are you sad because I won't suck your dick like a good little captive?" I push to my feet, instantly bringing myself chest to chest with him. The heat of his body bleeds through the material of my dress. The air crackles with tension and adrenaline thrums through my veins. I can't remember the last time I felt so alive. Ronan Cole may be a bastard, but his power is almost infectious and war with him...would be like nothing else.

"You underestimate me," he says. His hand skims my waist. "On *every* level." His fingers linger on the small of my back. A shiver tears down my spine before he tugs me flush against him and inches toward my neck. "Would be a pity to ruin such an exquisite face," he says before his teeth rake over my throat, and sink into my skin so hard that I gasp. And then, just like that, he releases me and takes a seat on the sofa again.

He's dangerous and powerful, and I'm drawn to him in the same way that an adrenaline junkie is to life threatening heights. I'll likely fall and die, but the trip down would be a rush unlike any other, so, I weigh my options. I could fight him tooth and nail for however long I'm here which could be infinite. Or...I could take this opportunity to get close to Ronan Cole, watch him, seduce him, work him. And when the time is right, I can either use him or kill him. I *can* work this to my advantage.

Chapter 8

Ronan

"Puppeteer" – MAX

Camilla glares at me.

Oh, I know she must hate me. She's easy to wind up—like a little toy. It does give me such a thrill when she tests me for I truly don't know how I'll react. Everything in my life is so predictable, and while that is what I need... it becomes tedious. And the worst damage she can do? Well, there *really* is nothing she can do as long as she's here, now is there? So, play with her I shall... "Dance for me, Camilla," I say with a smile.

A fire lights in her eyes and her nostrils flare. "Do I look like your own personal stripper?"

"You look like whatever I want you to be."

"Fuck. You!" She folds her arms across her ample chest. I've decided she's the most beautiful when she's angry.

"I said, dance."

She steps closer. "I will cut you, Russian."

"I'm quite fond of knives." I fight a groan as I remember how smoothly the blade slid over her thigh. A soft blush forms on her cheeks, and I can only hope she's thinking about it, too. On a sigh, I stand, and she takes a wary step back. "You make this so much harder than it has to be," I say as I grab her by the waist and pull her against my body. "You will do as I ask, either by choice or by force."

Her jaw sets as a sarcastic smile touches her lips. "I'm going to get off tonight picturing your dead, bloodstained body."

"How delightful." I force her to move with me, dancing. She obliges by pressing her body against mine and following my lead. The scent of her skin, the way she moves with those deadly curves, her palpable rage...she's an enticing creature. I spin her around before yanking her close again.

"I'll come so hard with my fingers buried in my pussy and you on my mind," she promises, her teeth graze over my neck.

She's filthy, and it does do things to me I rather enjoy. "And exactly how would you propose to kill me, Camilla Estrada?" I dip her, leaning over to skim my lips along her neck before I bite her. "I do hope it's brutal."

"Well, as you're so fond of knives... And is a kill even worth the effort without copious amounts of blood to show for it?" She shifts her thigh between mine, pressing it against my crotch. *Oh, she plays dirty.*

"You *would* look so pretty bathed in blood, Krasivaya." I fist her hair. "So very beautiful all in red." Adrenaline fires through me, and I want to test her boundaries because I feel she has very few.

"Red *is* my favorite color." She smiles and spins on her heels, placing her back to my front. Her hips roll against my hardening cock. She so badly wishes to seduce me, to watch me crumble. But I won't...

"Does it make you angry that I won't fuck you?" I brush her hair to the side of her neck and notice the hint of a large tattoo peeking from the top of her dress. And what a contrast it is against the satin material. She looks so elegant, yet she's utterly ruthless. Like a Lily of the Valley... "I do know how important having men fall at your feet is."

"Does it frustrate you that your tight control won't allow it?" She turns again, bringing her lips close to mine. "Does it make you want to let go for a night?" Her hand slides over my crotch as she quirks a brow.

"I don't mix pleasure and business and you, Camilla," I smirk "are very much business."

"Hmm." Her gaze drops to my lips. "And you, Ronan, are the enemy. But don't we always want the things we shouldn't?"

"Oh, but don't we?" I reach inside my pocket and grab my knife, pulling it out as I shove her against the bookcase. Her breath catches, and I smile before I slice across her chest. She gasps as a thin line of blood wells from the wound, trickling down perfectly over the slope of her breast. I swipe my finger through it, lift my hand to my lips, and touch the tip of my tongue to the drop of blood. "And I do so look forward to the day you're on your knees with my cock in your filthy little mouth," I whisper, shoving the knife back in my pocket as I let go of her.

She shoots a smug smile at me, and I snap my fingers. Within moments, Igor steps through the doorway and grabs Camilla by the elbow, escorting her from the room.

What a wonderful surprise this has turned out to be. I go to my desk and pull up the security camera footage on my laptop just in time to see Igor shove Camilla inside her room.

She stands frozen for a moment, and I just wonder what she's thinking. How angry she must be that I appear so immune to her charms. It's not long before she turns toward the camera, looks up, and flips me the bird. Clapping my hands, I laugh. *So festive and lively... And such pretty blood.* I fish the knife from my pocket and lay it on the desk, staring at the sharpened edge. Blood is very much a pleasure of mine. Something fascinating. But that is reason number one as to why I don't get my hands dirty. It's not good to mix pleasure with business. I learned early in my career that it's too easy to get carried away with, and I need things planned, calculated, controlled to ensure everything goes accordingly. However, one thing utterly excites me: Camilla won't be business for long—

"Sir," one of the guards steps into the room. "Anastasia Derevichi is at the front gate."

"I *wonder* why?" A smile curls my lips and I force the sordid thoughts of Camilla's red blood deep down. "Let her inside the grounds." I step around the guard and make my way down the hall. A servant is by the door waiting with my coat in hand. I take it and step onto the porch, pausing as a black car rounds the drive. A dusting of snow kicks up behind the tires when it comes to an abrupt stop.

The back door opens and Anastasia's long legs swing out. "Ronan," she says, her cheeks red, her face stained with mascara. "He knows."

Don't smile. "Who knows what, Ana?"

"Nikoli." She covers her mouth with her hand and sobs. "He knows about us!"

Of course he does, but I must pretend to be shocked, so I drag my hands through my hair and pace. "How?" I ask. "How does he know!"

"There were pictures..." I can see her pulse throbbing in her neck, and I delight at the sight. She's afraid of him, but she fears the wrong man.

Forcing a frown, I make my way down the steps and take Anastasia into my arms. "It will be alright." I press my lips to hers, losing myself in the theatrics of it all.

"What are we going to do?" she asks. "He threatened to kill you." *Oh, did he now? How wonderful!* How pleased

I am to hear that. While fucking Ana has been no hardship, I never fucked her for the sheer pleasure. I fucked her because of Derevechi. Because a woman's heart is her weakest point and hell hath no fury like a woman scorned. "I'm leaving him," she whispers.

"Don't be foolish." I step away and motion her toward the car. "He'll have us both killed if you leave." He won't, but she doesn't know that, and I want her to feel trapped.

I hold the door for her as I glance back at Camilla's window. She's standing beside the parted curtain, watching, and I must say, I couldn't have planned this better if I tried. Anastasia and I climb into the car, and as soon as the door is closed, I kiss her. Hard. Brutal, like all I need in the world is her, and in some ways, at this very moment that is true. She is my pawn to move and manipulate in order to take another king off the board.

Chapter 9

Camilla

"Firestarter" – The Prodigy

I watch Ronan get into the car with a skinny blonde and drive away. That woman wants him so badly; she might as well lie down on the snowy driveway and spread her mile-long legs. As if the man needs any more of an ego stroke.

One look at her and he had her right where he wanted her, and I'm just as helpless. Forced to remain his captive, powerless to do anything to help the business I built. Meanwhile, he's playing with me like one of his cheap whores. And I *let* him. I'm trying to play a game only he knows the rules to.

I nearly had him, until he had me.

I'm frustrated, I'm angry, and I want to fucking hurt him. I want to burn his perfect little life to the ground. The scene of him toying with me so easily replays in my mind, and my temper rises and rises with every passing second. It's his unending calm that annoys me, that perfect control that I can see he places such value upon. I smile at the thought of watching him snap. Watching a man such as him unleashed on the world—it would be beautiful and terrifying. He'd surely kill me, and then he'd have no leverage, no power over my brother *or* my cartel.

Just as he wants to break me, I want to break him, and by any means necessary. No one plays me.

I allow the rage to fill me, to take over in a way that usually ends in mass murder, and then I grab the mirror from the dressing table and throw it to the ground. The glass shatters, fragments scatter over the rug. My eyes shift to the new camera in my room, the little red light mocking me with each blink. I know his men can see me, so I pick up a big shard of glass and draw it over the inside of my wrist leaving a cut not deep enough to kill me. Just deep enough to cause a scene. The blood rushes to the surface, and I let it trickle onto the rug. For whatever reason, I think Ronan Cole wants me alive. It's not like I haven't given him every reason to kill me by now if that weren't the case. Maybe I can push him over the edge...

I tear apart the room, pulling curtains down, and flipping furniture over, and when the room is a complete mess, I sit on the edge of the bed, bleeding on the sheets. Almost on cue, footsteps pound down the hallway, and I tuck the big shard of glass beneath my thigh. The door swings open so hard it slams against the wall.

A man rushes in. He looks at me then around the room

before tossing his rifle over his back and hurrying to my side. When he's only a foot away, I leap up and slam the shard of glass into his neck. The jagged edges cut through my palm, but I don't care. I snatch the rifle from the strap at his back. More footsteps echo down the hall, and I point the gun at the doorway. Another guard steps into the room and I pull the trigger. *Bang*. He falls to the floor.

See how Ronan likes this shit, I think as I hurry out the door. I go through the house shooting anyone I see. At the bottom of the stairs I toss the empty rifle aside and grab a new one from the lifeless man at my feet. Five of Ronan's men are dead, and I haven't even reached the guard house yet. Bending over, I pat the man down for more weapons, and find two grenades. *Well, this is about to get a lot more interesting*. In his pocket are cigarettes and a lighter, both of which I take before stealing his thick coat and walking outside.

The howling wind wraps around me and I shiver violently. I slip the coat on and glance around, taking note of the men milling in and out of the guard house to the side of the drive. There are several SUVs parked in front of it, and I smile. Growing up, my brother and I would steal Papa's cars because they always had the keys in them. Certain occupations put you at a high risk of attack, and vehicles need to be ready to go. Ronan has a lot of enemies, so I'd assume those cars have keys in them. It takes me no time to run across the courtyard. I crouch next to one of the

SUVs and try the door. It opens and I reach up, dropping the sun visor. Keys fall onto the front seat. I grab them and jam them into the ignition. The engine coughs against the cold before sputtering to life. The sudden noise catches the attention of a few guards.

Ramming the rifle through the steering, I jam the accelerator down and wedge it into place. The engine roars and the tires scream. The guards are now jogging toward me, so I hurry to pull the pins from the two grenades and toss them onto the front seat before I slide the gear in to drive. I leap out of the way when the car takes off straight toward the guard house. It collides with the brick building, the engine whining as the wheels continue to spin. Then... *Boom.* An enormous wall of fire flashes, blinding me and knocking me off my feet. The angry blaze engulfs the car and the front of a building. Smoke rises into the sky. Dust settles, and Ronan's men look like broken dolls scattered over the courtyard. *He can eat shit.* Grinning, I push to my feet and walk over to one of the unconscious men. I remove the scarf from his neck, shred a strip of material from it, and wrap it around my cut wrist. Then I hop onto the hood of a car, taking one of the stolen cigarettes from my pocket and lighting it as I bask in the destruction. The heat from the roaring fire caresses my skin like an old friend. The flames leap and twist, crawling through the house and consuming everything. The distant screams of the men trapped inside the burning rubble are like a symphony accompanying the crackling of burning wood. It's beautiful. Mother nature at her finest; her most destructive and merciless. Burning alive is a nasty way to go, I'd think. The pain of being set on fire is unrivalled by anything; and yet, to feel your own skin melting from your flesh, bubbling and blistering is almost purifying.

The crunch of tires over the snow comes from behind me followed by the screech of brakes. A door bangs shut, and awareness prickles up my spine. I know it's Ronan without even looking. Like I said, I can always sense a predator. Boots stomp through the snow, and I sit here smoking my cigarette, watching the fire.

A hand snatches my arm, dragging me from the hood of the car. Igor snarls at me before grabbing the back of my neck and shoving me toward Ronan like a damn prize. My heart pounds in my chest, that little fissure of anticipation blending to fear. I bite my lip on a smile, wondering just what he'll do. *This should be fun...*

Ronan's gaze drifts over my body. His eyes are completely unreadable. He holds up a single finger before he turns and glances at the destruction surrounding him. I swear, I see him fighting a smile before his gaze snaps back to mine and narrows. His hand drops to his side, and there's a tense moment of silence where all you can hear is the hissing of the fire.

"Igor," he says, his voice barely restrained. "Leave."

Igor's boots crunch through the snow as he walks

away.

Ronan circles me like a tiger stalking prey. My breathing picks up, misting in front of my face as I stand completely still. Honestly, I want his rage, I want his fury. I want to watch him lose that ice cool façade because *I* pushed him to it. He stops behind me. "You don't like the bonfire?" I ask, glancing over my shoulder at him.

He steps so close to me that he's literally breathing down my neck, and the sudden heat sends an involuntary tremor through my body. "Oh," he says, his fingers slowly dancing along my side as he steps in front of me, "I like fire very much." I lift the cigarette to my lips and his eyes focus on my bloodied wrist. "*And* blood."

"Well," I smile wryly, "we all have our vices."

"So very true." He plucks the cigarette from my fingers and tosses it to the ground before he fists my hair, yanking my head back. "Are you going to tell me why you set my guard house on fire?" he asks. His fingers tighten in my hair until my scalp burns with pain.

My gaze drops from his eyes to his perfect lips. I do so love these dangerous little games with him—not that I'd tell him that. "Because I can," I say. I tell myself that I'm doing this for a reason, a greater cause: to help my brother, to beat the Russian. But the truth is, I like this. I want to watch Ronan snap, to lose control and destroy everything in his own beautiful inferno. I want to dance in the flames with him and feel my skin peel away in the heat. I want to walk that fine line where power, life, and death all combine.

"And yet, you stayed." He smiles. "Like a good little captive."

I stayed. I could have taken a car and attempted to run, but his reach is infinite, his power unrivalled. Even if I made it back to Mexico, he would hunt me down, and I'm not equipped for a war on his scale. "Good, or just intelligent? There's no escaping you, Ronan, and I know that."

"Mm," he says, releasing my hair and trailing his fingers, one by one, down the back of my neck. "Smart little kitty."

Fire and smoke billow behind him, the flames reaching into the sky as if worshipping him like the god he thinks he is... like the devil he *really* is. "So, what now? Are you going to kill me?" I smile.

"For what?"

"I killed half your men." I lift a brow and point at the burning building. "Did you miss the fucking great fire on your front lawn?"

"If a woman could put them down like dogs, why would I want them?" He shrugs. "You did me a favor."

Damn. He's so ruthless, and the thought shamefully has my thighs clenching together. "Well then, glad to be of service," I say, sarcasm dripping from my tone.

"Ah," he swipes a finger over my lip, "and now you are learning your place."

I glare at him. "Careful, Russian, next time it will be

your house—with you in it."

And the switch flips. The smug smile disappears and his eyes flame, and suddenly his hand is on my throat. "Gods don't burn," he says, squeezing as he lifts me up. My feet dangle above the ground as I flail in his hold. I scratch at his hand, and his grip only grows tighter. "Empty threats make you weak," he says. "I am not Jésus. I am not any man you've known. You may not fear death, but you should fear me." I'm choking under his brutal grasp, fighting for a breath as my lungs burn and my ears ring. A sick smile works over his lips, and he drops me to the ground. I gasp, rubbing against my throat as I scoot away from him.

He points to the raging fire behind me. "That is nothing more than a temper tantrum from a spoiled child. You are powerless to yourself, therefore you are weak."

His words burrow under my skin, worming their way into my mind and gnawing away at my flaws. I fight with myself, unable to say anything while his eyes dance with humor. He knows he just won. I burned his guard house to the ground and somehow I'm the one who looks weak. *What the fuck?* I push to my feet and storm off, dusting the snow from my palms as I go. His laughter soars over the sizzling flames and it makes me all the more angry. *Weak! I'll show him weak!*

Chapter 10

Ronan

"Hands on the Bible" - Local H

That time, I felt her heartrate pick up.

Excitement swirls around me as I watch her storm off. She fascinates me the way, I assume, a collector is fascinated by a rare specimen. She's something I've never seen before, magnificent. Exotic. Endangered...

I trudge toward the house admiring the crimson blood splatter on the snow. A few men lie here and there slumped on the steps. *Such carnage.* The foyer doors swing open to a bloodbath and I sigh. Bodies lay scattered across the marble. The blood laced scent of death hangs in the air, and I breathe it in, closing my eyes as I revel at the thought of her massacring these men like an angel of death. My pulse thrums with delight.

A throat clears. Igor stands at the top of the stairwell surveying the scene of death that lay before him. "She's angry," he says without emotion.

"Yes." I smile as I step over a man with a bullet hole in the middle of his head. "She is."

"Are you going to kill her?"

"She'll calm down," I say, and Igor lifts an eyebrow. I motion for him to follow me as I head toward my office. "Has the meeting been set up?"

"Yes, boss."

Humming, I make my way down the hall. The glow of the fireplace catches my attention when I step into my office. I cross the room and stop in front of the roaring fire, dragging in the scent of burning timbers. I hear Igor come in behind me, but I don't turn around. "What time are we to arrive?" I ask.

"Midnight."

I focus on the flames dancing over the logs. The wood crackles and splits, sending a flash of heat across my face, and a soft smile shapes my lips. Camilla is fire in every essence. Most people fear fire, but she has become it. Her beauty is in her destruction, rampant and hot. Her existence is grounded in the sole purpose to destroy. The very air she breathes turns into a sweet ecstasy that feeds her, makes her burn brighter—

"Ronan?" Igor interrupts my thoughts. I've been so lost in the fire, in my thoughts that I've not heard a thing he's said.

"What?"

"What do you want me to do with her?"

"Nothing." I dust ash from my sleeve and shrug. "And reiterate to the rest of the men, they are not to harm her. No matter what she tries."

"But she just—"

"Don't question my decisions, Igor. Now, tell her to get bathed and dressed. She'll be going with us to meet Anton." I dismiss him with a wave of my hand.

Camilla is too unpredictable, and for that reason alone I should kill her, but until I find her boring I'll let her live. I watch the flames dance in front of me for a moment longer before turning and taking a seat at my desk. Calls are made, arranging the next shipment of ammunition to be delivered outside of East London. Of course I must touch base with my account and have payments sent to assassins—all the trivial things that accompany my job—and when it's a quarter to ten, I push up from my chair.

On my way through the house, I think of how pretty Camilla would look draped on my arm at all those drab political meetings. All the men would envy me, and so I will take her tonight to test the waters. Anton is no one of importance really. No matter what fuss she makes, he'll still wriggle under my thumb like a maggot. I stop outside her room, adjusting my cufflinks before I shove the doors open. And just as I assumed, she's not ready. Why would she be? Instead, she's sprawled across the bed with a book in her hand, still dressed in her killing spree clothes. *Oh, don't you look so beautiful in your blood-stained clothes?*

The door slams shut behind me, but she doesn't acknowledge my presence. As though she's not a care in this world, she turns the page and sweeps her dark hair to the side. That's when I notice the blood splatter on her neck I take a breath, suppressing the thought of how I could fuck her.

I clap my hands and she jumps on the bed. "You're not dressed," I say.

"It's late." She sighs. "Why do I need to get dressed?"

"You were *told* to get dressed."

"You're a fucking delight tonight. Where, pray tell, am I going?" She rolls her eyes before she sits up.

"Get. Dressed."

"Are we going hiking through the woods? Going to a party? What would you like me to wear, *Russian*?"

My lips quirk up as I head to the closet. I grab a dress from the rack and toss it at her. "This will be fine."

"You're not even going to give me a hint of where we're going?" Her gaze skirts over my face, and she smiles.

I snap my fingers. "Put on the dress."

"Oh, I see. You're having to watch me because the men you hire are too shitty to do it."

I glance at my watch before taking her by the wrist and dragging her to the edge of the bed. "I ordered them not to. Now, put on the damn dress." I groan as I let her go.

"Well, basic self-preservation should override your orders."

"I don't have time for your chit-chat. Get dressed before I do it for you."

A wild spark dances in her eyes, and she pushes to her knees on the bed, bringing herself face to face with me. *Such a fun thing to play with*, I think as I ball the neckline of her dirty dress in my fists and tug. The thin material rips down the middle and she loses her balance. Her eyes flash. Her palm flies to my chest as she steadies herself. Much to my delighted surprise, she is completely naked underneath that dress. Her dark nipples tighten, her chest rises in one, uneven swell, and I struggle to restrain the animalistic urge gnawing through me. Begging me to throw her down and spread her legs apart.

"Get," I place my nose inches from hers, "dressed."

"Oh, Ronan." Her fingers trail from the collar of my shirt to my bare throat, and I clench my jaw as a flash of heat fires over me. "Such a model of self-control," she says, biting at her lip. "Shame."

She's nearly unbearable like this. "Perhaps you prefer being dragged out into the cold, naked?"

She scoots closer on her knees. Her breasts brush my shirt when she leans in, and I fight a groan. "Anyone would think you don't like me naked," she breathes against my lips. Lust bubbles beneath my skin. My cock swells. My fingers twitch at my side, aching to swipe over her bare pussy. And while she may be toeing a thin line of seduction, so can I.

I sweep my lips over hers then trail them across her

cheek on my way to her ear. "I don't like my women easy," I whisper. Smiling, I take a step back, grab the dress from the floor, and toss it at her.

"And I like a man who takes what he wants. Like I said, shame."

I chose to ignore her, allowing her the last word simply to hurry this process along. She slips into the dress, tugging it over her curves before walking to the mirror. The dress dips low in the back, revealing a large, intricate tattoo. Dark angels and demons, a scene of macabre violence. Her soul is dark, and such a contradiction to her beautiful exterior. Alluring and deadly, such a lethal combination. She stares at her reflection and gathers her hair to the side. *Ah! The blood splatter*. I go into the bathroom and wet a washcloth, checking the time once more before I step back into the room. Camilla turns from the mirror, glaring at me as I approach her. I sweep her hair behind her shoulder.

"As pretty as this is..." I say, cleaning the dried blood from her neck. "I'm afraid it's not appropriate attire for the occasion."

The neon light of Club Hades bounces off the window as the car loops around the building, parking between a Rolls Royce and a Mercedes. Igor climbs out and heads toward the back entrance. A mound of snow falls from the eave when he opens the door and disappears inside. Several of my men are already waiting inside the club. Some are positioned precariously on the rooftops of surrounding buildings, but a man such as myself can never be too cautious.

Sighing, I glance at the stock report pulled up on my phone. *Are you sure you want to sell 2,000,000 shares of Valiant Oil?* I click Yes before closing the browser and slipping my phone back into my suit pocket. This sudden sale should give the stock market a nice little jolt, and then when all the other companies panic and sell, I'll swoop in like a vulture and seize them all. After all, the more companies I own, the more men I control, the more money I have to buy off the right people.

The driver hops out of the car, and I glance through the window at Igor now lurking in the open doorway. My door opens and I step out into the cold night. Camilla climbs out behind me, her eyes shifting in every direction. *Oh, the fearless Camilla appears to be spooked.* "You seem uneasy," I say, adjusting my suit jacket as we approach the building.

"No shit." Her breath turns to a puff of fog in the frigid air, and she quickly wraps her arms around herself on a shiver. "I'm surrounded by Russians, walking into whatever fun you've lined up, and I don't have a gun."

"A gun," I laugh. "Why on earth would you need a gun? You're with me."

She gives me a quick once over when we stop in front of the doorway. "I'm sorry, Russian. I didn't realize you were bullet proof. I'll be sure to stay behind you then." Igor steps to the side and we walk into a dimly lit hallway. "At least tell me you have a gun," she whispers.

"No." I feel her tense next to me.

"Great," she grumbles. "Just fucking great."

"I don't need a gun."

"If you say you're god right now, I'm going to hurt you."

We continue down the hallway, and with each step, she bristles beside me. Oh, how her nervous energy sends a surge of adrenaline buzzing through me. In the world she grew up in, violence was the way to obtain power, but this is not the same world. I straighten my jacket when we approach the last door in the hall. "Don't speak unless I ask you to," I say, placing my hand on the knob, and she rolls her eyes.

I am so very excited to see how she reacts...

Chapter 11

Camilla

"Wild Thoughts" – DJ Khaled, Rihanna

The door opens and I'm lead into a small, dimly lit room. A man in a suit sits at the lone table, his face cast in shadow. The door clicks shut and he jolts at the sound. Ronan crosses the room and pulls out a chair, gesturing for me to sit before he takes a seat beside me. The man anxiously drags his hand through his graying hair, then adjusts his red silk tie. He looks like any well-presented guy, and yet somehow, sitting across from Ronan, he seems so small and drab.

"Mr. Cole..." The man coughs.

"Ronan, please," he says with a smile that oozes charisma.

"I didn't expect to see *you*." His face adopts a sheen of sweat as tension draws heavy lines on his brow.

"With such an *important* task at hand, I thought it prevalent to discuss the terms of our agreement in person."

The man nods so sharply I'm afraid his head might fall off. Jesus, this guy is like a dog barking 'how high, how high'.

"The email has been sent," his voice shakes.

"Good. Very, very good." Ronan drums his fingers over the table, his eyes studying the man in a way that makes even me anxious. I can see the man sweating, swallowing. His fear is palpable, swirling through the air like a dense fog. "Now," Ronan says, "the terms. I can make it so that that email goes away forever, however, defy me, and it will resurface." Ronan's lips curl on each side, the master playing with his puppets. "Prison doesn't suit you, Anton. All you must do is bend to my every whim. After all, that is a small price to pay to be Russia's next Prime Minister." He pauses, picking an invisible piece of lint from his sleeve. "Remember, you turn your back on this agreement, and you turn your back on me. And I am not a man you want to have your back to."

Rumors about Ronan Cole run rampant in the criminal world, and his name comes with a very healthy dose of respect, but I had no idea he was pulling political strings. This isn't the way our world works. The legal and the illegal are two different sides of the same coin, together and yet always opposing. The two don't go hand in hand. One may use the other temporarily—cartels may buy off police officers, governments may even work with cartels—but the end game is always the same: to dupe and win. There's something about this that is very different. Ronan is controlling the flow of power itself. He's corrupting the political system that would seek to destroy him, and if you think about it he wouldn't have to bring the law to his side. He could *be* the law. This is the bigger picture, and as I stand back and watch him, I see it in all its glory. I see what he sees.

The two men stare at each other, and Ronan commands every inch of space in the room as though he's physically impressing his will on everyone in it. Tension winds across the back of my neck, prickling my skin. It riles me, but it terrifies Anton. I can almost see him shrinking into his chair, cowering like the little pet Ronan has turned him into, and *this* is a man who is to hold power? Ironic that he should be so utterly weak.

Anton nods and Ronan stands without a word, holding out his hand to me. A hypnotic dominance pours from him as our eyes lock. I want him dead, but I can't deny the draw, the fascination that surrounds him. I can't help but respect and crave a man who commands this kind of power like an addiction, like a sickness. He takes my hand and energy hums through me, buzzing over my skin in the form of goosebumps. As soon as I stand, I snatch my hand away from him. *Focus. I need to focus.* His fingers graze the small of my back as he guides me from the room.

I keep walking, refusing to turn and look at him. Awareness tugs at my mind, every instinct demanding that I adjust my position because, as he said, he is not a man you want to have your back to.

"So tense, little kitty," he laughs.

And for the first time since I met Ronan, I don't say anything. I have no sharp come back, no sarcastic retort. I'm on unstable ground right now, and I need to remind myself why I'm here and who he is—the enemy. *Play the prisoner, seduce the devil, and kill him. Simple.* There is no room for anything else because I refuse to lose to him.

His hand lands on my shoulder before he spins me around and slams my back against the cold wall. Those blue eyes swim with cruel promises as his hands roam my curves. Soon enough, I'm trapped between his body and the wall. He shoves his leg between my thighs, spreading them apart. I can't breathe. All I can do is feel him...everywhere. He pins my hands above my head, and a smirk pulls at his lips as he inches his mouth close to mine. So close I can taste his breath. "Is something wrong?" he whispers against my lips.

Closing my eyes, I rest the back of my head against the wall. I fight every instinct screaming at me to grind against his hard thigh, to let him fuck his way inside me until he is all I feel. I hate him, and yet that very hate seems to act as an aphrodisiac. I open my eyes, and stare straight back at him. "No."

His tongue skims my lip before he shoves away from me. "Good, girl," he says on a wink before walking off. *God, I hate him.*

I follow him outside and into the waiting limo. The

heaters kick up when the car pulls away from the club, and I watch the snow-covered streets pass by in a blur, thinking of all the ways I could kill him...

"I have some rather *unsavory* business to handle," he says. I turn to find him staring through his window. "Surely, you won't mind?"

"And there was me believing everything you do is unsavory."

"Refined. Unsavory." He laughs, and I find that deep chuckle sexier than I should. "Mostly one in the same really," he says.

We drive until the shiny buildings of central Moscow turn to crumbling tower blocks and boarded-up shops. The car slows in front of a building. A metal roller door takes up most of the front, and the sign above the awning has a string of Russian letters blinking beside a neon martini glass.

"This looks like a nice place," I say, wrinkling my nose as the car turns into the parking lot.

"Much like your beloved Juarez." A mocking smile dances over his lips. "Do you feel at home?"

I glare at him. "Juarez is hot, and has decidedly more hookers—"

"Deplorable at best."

"She's a thorn in America's side at least." I glance through the window. "This place..."

"Do you like to hear yourself talk?" He arches a brow as he casually checks his phone.

"You're such a dick." I roll my eyes. "Are we just sitting here, or are we going to get out and start dodging heroin needles?"

The back door to the bar opens, light spilling across the ice-covered sidewalk. A man waves from the doorway and, like clockwork, Ronan's door is opened for him. He steps out and I follow him to the back entrance.

"Stay close," he orders as we step inside.

The aroma of beer, mildew, and urine is distinct. *Lovely*. The walls are covered with wooden wainscoting, and tacky brass fixtures hang from the ceiling. Pub tables are scattered about with unlit candles in the center. Ronan leads me through the empty bar to the hallway, and into a much larger room.

A row of men dressed in suits sit along the wall, and a thick cloud of smoke lazily drifts through the air. Igor and another of Ronan's guards stand in the middle of the room across from an empty chair. Two disheveled-looking men sit directly in front of them, hands bound and bags covering their heads.

Ronan pulls a cigar from his pocket, making a slow show of lighting it as he takes a seat. One puff, and he braces his elbows on his thighs, staring across the room at the row of men. The silence in the room is deafening. I can practically see them holding their breath, waiting to see what he'll do. I duck my chin and try to hide my smile.

"Kristoff," Ronan says, the smoke slowly seeping

through his lips. "Take the bags off."

The man beside Igor steps forward and pulls the bags off their heads. One man appears to be middle-aged, his salt and pepper hair thinning. He stares nervously at the baby-faced man beside him.

Ronan glances at me as he pulls a drag from his cigar. "Do you know what these two men thought they could do?" I lift a brow. *Is he serious right now?* "They thought they could defy me," he says, shaking his head. "Rebel against *my* Bratva. Inconceivable, really."

"Dissension is such a disease," I say, placing my hand on Ronan's shoulder. He's testing me somehow, I know it. Smiling, he grabs my hand and kisses over my knuckles as though he's proud of me. The worst part of it is—I like it.

He lets go of my hand and directs his attention toward the men. "Honestly, Marat," Ronan says, "the most tragic part of it is that you brought your son down with you. Tsk. Tsk." Another pull from his cigar, a cloud of smoke swirling in the air. "You signed Victor's death warrant." Ronan snaps his fingers, and Igor holds out a gun. Marat looks at it, sweat visibly beading his brow. "Which means *you* get to kill him."

"No," Marat says, snarling. "I won't do it. If you want to kill my boy, do it yourself. Get your hands dirty for once."

"You do understand that if I kill him it will be so much worse." Ronan sighs. "If you love Victor, I'm sure you'll find the humanity in killing him yourself." It's brutal and twisted, but effective leadership requires swift punishments for those who rise against you. Punish one man properly and few will ever try to defy you again. I know this well.

"You go against the rules, Ronan. You're power hungry. Inhumane. Your father would be disgusted," Marat shouts, his eyes flashing with rage and fear.

"Ah, come now." Ronan throws his head back on a laugh. "We all know what happened to my father." He laughs again, and the men to the side of the room shift uncomfortably. "I'm not an unreasonable man," he says, handing his cigar to Igor and adjusting his cufflinks. "I'll make a deal with you, Marat. Shoot your son now, and your wife and granddaughter live. Don't shoot him and, well..." Ronan takes his cigar back and puffs away with a grin.

Marat's eyes lock on the gun in Igor's hand, and his jaw tenses. "No."

"Please, father," his son begs. I guess the granddaughter Ronan is threatening is Victor's child, and he wants her to live. Perhaps I should feel a modicum of sympathy for these men, but I don't. Everyone in this room is tainted. The normal ethics of humanity do not apply here because we all willingly traded our souls for this lifestyle. As for Marat and his son...well, they didn't just sell their soul to the devil, they then tried to overthrow him. Dangerous, dangerous games.

"Tick, tock," Ronan says.

Marat tentatively takes the gun and lifts it in his trembling hand, glaring at Ronan with wild eyes. Suddenly, he aims the gun at Ronan. "Let my son go!" he shouts.

I swear the temperature in the room drops. Everything goes silent, as though time itself stands still. Ronan's jaw ticks, his nostril's flare. Nothing exists outside of Ronan's rage filling every corner of the room. If this bastard gets shot, I'm stuck here with a load of Russian Bratva. Ronan may be the enemy but, in this case, I'd rather be his captive than their play thing.

Well, fuck.

Chapter 12

Ronan

"Click Click Boom" – Saliva

Click. Click. Click. Guns cock all around me, and the room brims with a crackling tension. Marat angles the gun, and I hold up my hand on a smile. "Wait!" I say. Marat's eyes widen, the tremor in his hand grows more violent. Sweat trickles down his temples. "Pull the trigger Marat. Go ahead," I dare before I take a long drag from my cigar.

"Ronan," Camilla says with a hiss.

"Yes, Krasivaya?" I direct my attention at her, my hand still raised at my guards.

"Kill him," she says through clenched teeth. Her eyes flick nervously to Marat.

"I don't get my hands dirty." I shrug. "It's a rule I strictly abide by."

She drags her hand through her hair. "Not the time." *Oh, she's worried...interesting.*

There's the distinct click of the hammer releasing, and

I turn back to Marat with a displeased frown. The gun was empty. It was all just a game for my entertainment, a little psychological torture if you will. Of course, Igor was going to shoot them both, but now...

"Do you really think I would hand you a loaded gun?" I ask Marat. Adrenaline-laced blood pulses through my jugular. Red distorts my vision. I can handle many things, but this—I cannot. How dare such a man point a gun at me when I am granting him a mercy? Slowly, I push up from my chair and step toward Marat, pacing in front of him. The feral beast inside me begs to slice his throat. It screams for bloodshed and violence. But I will not give into that craving because I would like it too much. This is business, and yet...I glance over my shoulder at Camilla, and curiosity dances around my screaming demons. She's so unhinged. So uncontrolled. I would never in my wildest dreams predict what this little hellhound would do, so maybe I should unleash her.

"Kill them," I say, stubbing my cigar out on Marat's cheek, a pained hiss leaving his lips. "Make it savage, Krasivaya."

I cross the room and take a seat. Camilla's heels click over the concrete floor, and she stops in front of Marat. My gaze drifts over her curves as I wait, as I think of all the possibilities.

"I'll need a few things from the bar," She turns to face me, and I nod. "Igor," she says on her way out of the room, "be a doll and make sure Marat gets a good show, would you?"

Igor grabs Marat and forces him to his knees in front of his son. The room is silent apart from Victor's muffled sobs. Seconds later, Camilla steps through the doorway carrying a kerosene candle from the bar and a dirty dish towel. Her hips sway with each step as she crosses the room. My chest tightens with anticipation when she stops in front of me. Her eyes gleam, and she slowly leans over, placing one hand on my thigh as the other trails the lapel of my coat. Smirking, she grabs the lighter from my breast pocket, flips the lid, and flicks the flint. The flame dances between us, and I catch a spark of madness in her exotic eyes. She's like an artist staring at a blank canvas while envisioning all the beautiful possibilities. With a flick of her wrist, she snaps the lighter closed, snuffing out the flame before turning away.

Victor whimpers when Camilla steps in front of him. She unscrews the top of the candle before dumping the oil onto one end of the towel. *How promising!*

"I do love fire," she says, lifting the rag to Victor's face. He clamps his mouth shut and she circles behind him, dragging the towel over his cheek. "The power, the way it decimates and cleanses everything it touches." She kicks the back of his legs, and he drops to his knees in front of Marat with a grunt. "It's almost spiritual," she says and grabs Victor's hair, yanking his head back and pinching his nose.

He thrashes about as she hovers over him with a sadistic smile. Finally, he gasps for breath and Camilla crams the towel inside his mouth. He grunts and groans, fighting against her as she forces it deeper. She flips the lighter open with a click, the flame sparking to life over the end of the cloth. His eyes widen and he flops onto his back, flailing wildly as the small blue flame creeps over the material. I anxiously watch, waiting for the fire to meet the kerosene, and suddenly a bright red flame flashes to life. Camilla continues to hold his nose, forcing him to inhale the flames licking around his face. Fascination swims in her eyes for a moment, and when she seems bored with it all, she releases him.

She's so ruthless. So utterly savage that my heart leaps in my chest.

A morbid symphony fills the room as Marat's sobs mix with Victor's muffled screams. Camilla turns her attention to Marat, stroking her finger over his cheek. "Shhh," she says, as she circles behind him. Cupping his jaw, she slides her hand around the back of his head before violently snapping his neck to the side. And my, the crack that echoes around the room... Marat's body topples to the floor with a thud, and then she walks away with a smile.

Depravity swirls around her like an angry storm. *She is magnificent.*

She flippantly waves her hand in Victor's direction. "That one will take a while to die. Might want to shoot him if you have somewhere to be."

I fight to contain myself as I turn to the group of men on the side of the room. "Gentlemen, just a reminder as to why you should not rebel against me. The consequences are dire." With a clap of my hand, I push up from my chair. "Well, that's enough excitement for one night. Igor, shoot him."

There's the quick bang of gunfire, and then I leave the building with Camilla at my side.

Chapter 13

Camilla

"River of Fire" – In This Moment

The smell of charred skin lifts from my coat when we step outside, and I can't pretend I don't relish in it. I like fire—too much. I once feared it, but it cleansed me, molded me, created what I am today.

Ronan holds the car door open for me—*so he can open doors*—and I slide across the seat, thinking about what just happened. That punishment is one I reserve for those who have wronged or betrayed me in the worst way. Inhaling flames until they scorch your lungs and suffocate you must be a horrible way to go.

I didn't know those men, and they did nothing to me, but they served a purpose: to get to Ronan Cole. Ronan has a weakness for violence and a hunger for retribution. I can see it in his eyes: the need, the drive so much like my own. But unlike me, he keeps his under lock and key, suppressed beneath that fine veneer of his.

He asked me to exact a punishment, to be brutal, and so I unleashed the worst parts of myself. I allowed my addiction to the most basic form of human power—taking another person's life— to consume me. For him. To get to him. I want to feed his weakness so that I become it; unhinging all his darkest secrets until he's ripe for the picking. I want to destroy Ronan Cole, but I also want to embrace his depravity. His darkness reaches out to mine, and they blend and swirl together in a void of our own making. I could so easily be the monster he wants me to be. After all, it's not exactly hard, I am my papa's daughter.

The dark night creeps past the window, and I turn to glance at Ronan. The blue glow from the phone in his hand casts shadows across his face. "Would you like to come to dinner with me tomorrow evening?" he asks before he looks up from the phone.

I frown. "What?"

"Would you like to join me for dinner tomorrow? I'm only asking to be polite, you really have no choice in the matter."

"You know," I roll my eyes, "you could have pretended not to be a dick for two point five seconds."

"Why pretend?"

"You're right," I sigh. *This is perfect.* I'll take any opportunity to get closer, but I can't make it too easy. "Why do you want me to go?"

His finger brushes my cheek. "You'll make me the envy

of so many men at the dinner. I do like to be envied..."

"And there was me thinking you were above such things, Russian."

"Appearances are everything."

"What's in it for me?" I bite my lip.

"Pretending you have a choice in the matter."

I lift a brow. I'll go to learn more about him. Knowledge is, after all, power. "Fine. Where are we going?"

"Moscow."

"Not like I have any other offers," I mumble.

"And I can't very well introduce you as the *former* leader of the Juarez cartel. I think CEO of the Bank of Venezuela should suit you nicely."

I shake my head. "Why a bank?"

"It's a business dinner, and I own many, many banks."

"Of course you do."

He studies my face like he's waiting for the ball to drop. "And don't be stupid, Camilla."

I fold my arms over my chest. "Again. Dick." The truth is, I'm intrigued by his world, and dare I say it, him. Besides, what else am I going to do? Sit in that room fuming? I refuse to give up hope and just accept this fate as his prisoner. I will kill him, and I'm not going to achieve that from behind a locked door. If possible, I need a modicum of his trust, but I'm not sure Ronan has any trust to give. It's why he's so powerful.

But the second he gives me an inch; I'll go a mile to

fucking destroy him.

Chapter 14

Ronan

"That Dress" – The Pale White

The sun sets on the horizon as the car winds through the busy streets of Moscow.

I send a text to Igor: *Have Camilla here in five minutes*, then I toss my head back against the leather seat, already bored to tears from the party I'm about to attend. My bank endorses Derevechi, and as a hard and fast supporter, I'm expected to show my face at these events. Sometimes a photograph of a handshake will buy your innocence, after all.

The car rolls to a stop outside the restaurant, and I wait for the driver to open the door. When I step out, cameras flash. I smile and wave, watching as Nikoli and Anastasia walk to the entrance of the restaurant. Her gaze drifts to me. A deep pout settles on her face as she clings to her husband. Even from here I can see the longing. Women are such predictable creatures: make them believe there's something they can't have and they crave it, they seek it out like an addict searching for one more hit. Poor Anastasia, if only she realized there's a fine line between addiction and death.

I shake hands with the politicians, with the other elite, and then I'm whisked inside. The restaurant is a flurry of activity. Waiters and waitresses scurry about, hoping to make the tip of a lifetime. The entire room is filled with men in suits, beautiful women with the perfect smile.

I weave my way between the tables, looking for my name card, and a man blocks the path in front of me. "Mr. Cole," he says, holding his hand out to shake mine. I take it and nod. "I'm Rick VanHeussen, Parliament member one-hundred nine." He grins. I want to roll my eyes, but appearances are important when you're trying to deceive.

"Very nice to meet you," I say.

"And I just wanted to thank you for your bank's charitable contribution to Skveya Orphanage."

I spot my name card on the far table, and offer another smile. "Bless the little children," I say before patting over his back and excusing myself to my seat.

Derevichi's table is next to mine, and I smile at him as I sit next to Anton. Prime Minister Vasily is at Anton's other side discussing some foreign exchange policy, but I doubt Anton is hearing a word. His face is glistening with sweat, and he keeps shifting anxiously in his seat. One's conscience can be such a burden...I grab the napkin from the table and lay it over my lap. "You look, ill, Anton," I say. "I hope you're not coming down with the flu. It's dreadful." I smile mockingly before lifting a glass of water to my lips.

"Ronan. A pleasure," Vasily says, reaching across the table to shake my hand. "I was just telling Anton that..." His gaze veers off to the side of the room. "My!" he says, and I turn in my chair. *Camilla.* Each sway of her hips is a form of seduction, and the white dress I ordered her to wear is striking against her dark skin. She oozes sexuality and every single man in this room takes note of her.

I turn my attention back to the table. Vasily is still gawking with his mouth open. I feel her step behind me.

"Gentlemen," Camilla says, delicately plucking her name card from the table. "I believe I have the pleasure of your company." She unbuttons the fur stole, undraping it from her shoulders, and casually hangs it across the back of her chair. My gaze drops to her chest, admiring the way her breasts strain against the bodice with each breath. Every man at the table shifts in his seat, and I'm certain they're undressing her with their eyes. Camilla is not just beautiful, she's stunning. The perfect image of fantasy. The kind of woman none of the men at this table—aside from myself—would ever have a shot in the dark with.

"Ronan Cole," I say, extending my hand to her.

She turns to me, her gaze flicking over my body. "Camilla Estrada," she caresses the words with her accent, making something as simple as her name sound exotic and sexy. "From Venezuela Financial."

I take her hand and bring it to my lips. I kiss gently over her knuckles, my eyes locked with hers as I arch a single brow. "What a pleasure to finally meet you."

"It's a pleasure to do business with you, Mr. Cole."

I trail my fingers over the inside of her palm, glancing at Anastasia's table. Ana is watching my every move. Worrying. I drop Camilla's hand and look up at the men left dumbfounded at her beauty. "Ms. Estrada's business has recently become an *asset* of mine," I say, smirking at her. "Ms. Estrada, this is the Prime Minister of Russia, Vasily Minovichi."

She turns to face Vasily. He holds out his hand to her, his cheeks flushing. "A pleasure," she says, shaking his hand. I point out the other inconsequential people seated at the table. Camilla nods and smiles, playing her part perfectly. After all, I can't very well introduce her as my hostage. It would put a nasty stain on my image.

And so the dinner begins with hors d'oeuvres and talks of politics and money. Every man in a pissing contest to impress Camilla while I simply sit and watch, throwing in an opinion every now and then for conversation's sake. After the plates are cleared, I glance at my watch and excuse myself to the restroom. Much to my delight, when I come out, Anastasia is waiting in the corridor. I stop midstride, lifting a brow as I adjust my jacket. "What are you doing, Ana?"

"I can't stand not seeing you. Nikoli is gone this

weekend. Stay with me," she pleads, nervously glancing down the hallway.

"You know that's not wise." I check the time again.

"I don't care." She hesitates, placing her hand on my arm. I promptly remove it. "Ronan, who is that woman?"

A slight jolt of pleasure courses through me. What a delightful bonus this is. Anastasia is bothered by Camilla, but of course she is. "A business partner." My lips quirk up. "Jealousy doesn't suit you," I say and turn to walk off,

"Ronan, I..."

I keep walking, my dismissiveness wounding her deeply, I'm sure.

Camilla is talking to Vasily when I return to the table. He's eating from the palm of her hand, hanging on her every word. She laughs at something he says casually placing her hand on his arm. Frowning, I take my seat and check my watch again. *Any minute...* I slide my hand under the table and over Camilla's thigh, squeezing. She tenses, clearing her throat as a fake smile falls from her lips. She has no idea how eventful this dinner is about to become. I do enjoy surprises.

I lean into her. "Scoot closer to me," I say quietly.

Before she can react, the window behind the table shatters. Camilla clutches my arm, people scream. The *pop, pop, pop* of gunfire echoes through the room, and Vasily's head hits the table with a thud. Blood splatters the table cloth, and I fight a smile at the sight. People duck beneath tables, some take off running, Anton faints, and chaos ensues. All the while Camilla sits here stoically, unfazed by the blood coating her chest. I must say, the red splatter looks magnificence over her white satin dress.

"Do try to look a little shocked," I whisper in her ear. "You are a banker, after all." I take a napkin from the table and dab at the brain matter stuck to her cheek. Amidst the screams, people running around, dishes breaking, I allow a smidge of a grin. "I chose white for you just for this reason. Blood looks so festive over something so clean."

"You enjoy this, don't you?" she asks with a tilt of her lips.

"*Immensely.*"

Body guards quickly surround us. I stand, smoothing my jacket before I hold out my hand to Camilla. She glances at me, raising an eyebrow as she places her hand in mine. When she stands, I grab the fur stole from her chair and leisurely place it around her shoulders. "Don't want to be cold," I say. The Presidential Security Service swarm past as we make our way to the doors. A crowd has already gathered at the front of the restaurant. I take a breath and close my eyes, forcing my jaw to go slack to feign shock. "Lean into me." I wrap my arm around her waist and tug her close. "Pretend to be distraught, you are, after all, covered with Vasily's brain."

"This was such a nice dress," she sighs before burying her face in my shoulder.

The doors swing open to a flurry of excitement and horror, to police cars screeching to a halt. We stumble onto the snow-covered sidewalk and Paparazzi rush us, firing off a hundred questions. I do enjoy the buzz such unexpected tragedies create.

A photographer snaps a picture of Camilla in her blood splattered dress. Playing the role of the protective male, I scowl at him and place my palm against her cheek, pulling her to my chest. She clutches my jacket and lets out a sob. "Please," I say, "no questions. We just..." I take a staggering breath. "We just need to pray for Russia."

Shaking my head, I move us away from the swarming crowd. The body guards surround us like a wall as I usher Camilla inside the waiting car. The door slams shut behind us, muting the chaos outside.

"You could have warned me," she says as she sits back in the seat and looks down at her dress. "Why spend money on Valentino only to ruin it?"

I laugh. "What else would you wear to an assassination?"

"Red?"

"But the white makes it look all the more dramatic." I smile. "A distraught woman dressed in Valentino, soaked with the Prime Minister's blood while Ronan Cole consoles her. What more could the press wish for?"

I watch the sparkle of excitement dance in her eyes as she stares at her blood-splattered chest. I've never met a woman so ruthlessly beautiful. A woman I would dare to think may possibly be a match to myself. *Possibly...* I take her hand and lift it to my lips, inhaling the metallic scent of blood that lingers on her skin. "A beautiful woman soaked in blood," I murmur over her knuckles. "It does do something to a man."

A bemused smile shapes her lips. "I thought you were averse to mess?"

"This..." I trail my finger over the red smudge on her collarbone, "this is not a mess." I streak the blood along her neck, then grab her hair and yank her head to the side. She gasps, her hands landing on my chest. "This is art," I whisper as I lean in and trail my tongue along the smeared blood, relishing in the taste of absolute power over her, over men, over everything.

Her palm slowly eases up the front of my jacket until her fingers trail the back of my neck. The car bumps over the uneven pavement. Our eyes lock. And here we are at a standoff. Lion versus lioness. The air crackles with a sort of tension much like the calm before the storm. *Which way shall the wind blow, Krasivaya?*

Her chest falls in ragged swells, and I tighten my hold in her hair in an attempt to ground myself. To regain control. I imagine what she would feel like naked and helpless, pinned underneath me. Slowly, I let her hair fall from my hand and ease back into the seat, directing my attention out the window.

On an exhale, she scoots to the other side of the car. It's such a dangerous game we're playing. Back and forth. Push and pull. Kill or let live... And if I'm honest, I don't know that I've enjoyed playing with someone like this before.

Within thirty minutes the car winds down my private road and stops at the front of the house. The driver opens my door, and I climb out, offering Camilla my hand. She takes it with a frown, and I pull her to her feet so hard that she staggers into my chest. There's a pause, and I drop her hand, skirting my thumb across her lip. The truth is, I crave her in the most depraved ways although I shouldn't. *I shouldn't* I think as I climb the stairs.

The butler greets me in the entranceway, taking my coat before stripping Camilla of her stole. "Arrange to have Ms. Estrada's dress dry cleaned, please," I say, and he nods before walking off.

"You must keep the cleaners busy," Camilla says.

A knowing smile crosses my lips. "You're welcome to roam about," I say, adjusting my cufflink. "Just try not to kill anyone."

"That's your job, Ronan."

Ah, Ronan. Not Russian. How civil of her. I make my way down the corridor and into the living room for my nightly ritual: a drink, a cigar, and the late evening news. After all, I do enjoy seeing what carnage I create each day. I settle onto the couch with a cigar in hand, and one of the servants turns the television on.

"—Minister Vasily was shot while attending a dinner to celebrate the upcoming election." Newsreels of people scurrying from the building flash across the screen, and there, in the corner of the frame is footage of Camilla clutched to my chest. So distraught. I grin. That dress did look striking... "At the time, there are no suspects, however they assume it may have been terrorists." *Always with the terrorists...* I light my cigar as I'm handed a glass of brandy. "The threat of nuclear war seems eminent as officials have discovered a laboratory in China suspected of housing radioactive materials used for Korean nuclear warheads... In financial news, the stock market plummeted after two million shares of Valiant Oil were sold. Brokers were in a frenzy as banks suffered massive withdrawals." I smile as I type out an email to my broker directing him to use twenty million dollars to buy while stocks are low.

"Boss?" Igor steps into the room and holds a phone up. "Ana..."

Rolling my eyes, I take a puff from my cigar, then place it in the ashtray as I motion him over. This entire ordeal is annoying at best, but taking out a President isn't easy work. I take the phone and press the receiver to my ear. "Yes," I say, my attention straying back to the television as Igor silently leaves.

"Ronan," Anastasia's voice comes over the line. "Thank heavens. I was worried about you."

"I'm fine," I say.

"It's terrifying. What if that had been you? I just can't..." Her endless rambling fades into the background as I watch the images of war on the screen. I can only imagine what the news will look like six months from now when my plan is in full swing. "Ronan?" she says, snapping my mind away from the television. "Isn't it terrible? Poor Vasily." I drag my hand down my face and shake my head, trying to force the aggravation away. "It's all just so barbaric."

"It is... Are you okay?" I ask, not that I care, but I must seem like I do.

"Just shaken." There's a slight movement in the doorway and I turn, watching Camilla step into the room. The silk robe she's changed into leaves little to the imagination. I do enjoy her little attempts at seduction, although her chances would have been higher had she not washed the blood from her chest. "You were so dismissive at the restaurant," Anastasia whines.

"We can't take chances, Ana. Nikoli..."

"Do you not want me?"

My eyes lock on Camilla. "Of course I want you," I whisper into the phone. Camilla's sinful hips sway with every step she takes across the room. When she stops in front of me, she takes the brandy from my hand. I watch her lips delicately touch the rim of the glass before she tips the drink back. "You have no idea how badly I want to fuck you," I say.

Camilla's eyes flicker, and she moves to the server in the corner of the room. I push up from the sofa and follow her, watching as she picks up the decanter and pours another drink.

"When can I see you again?" Ana asks.

"Soon." I stop behind Camilla and sweep her hair to the side, skimming my nose along her neck. Inhaling the intoxicating scent of her skin. "So soon."

"And what are you going to do, Ronan?" Ana whispers, so desperate for the attention. "Tell me what you'll do with me."

"I would ruin you." I press my lips to Camilla's neck. She leans against me, tilting her head to the side as her hand slides up my neck, her nails scratching into my hair. "Are you wet for me?" I ask.

"God, yes... Ronan." Anastasia moans, and I cradle the phone between my cheek and shoulder.

My dick swells with the thought of taking Camilla— of desecrating her. Those primitive urges bubble to the surface, and I surprise myself when I grab her by the hips, pressing my cock against her ass in a bid to have just a small taste. "I would fuck you so hard..." I groan next to her ear. Her fingers tighten in my hair, her back bowing. She wants me just as much as I want her, and oh what a prize this shall be. I spin her around, our eyes locking. "How wet are you right now?" She bites down on her lip, and I shove my knee between her legs, spreading them apart before I force her onto the sideboard. "How fucking wet?" I say into the phone, my eyes glued to Camilla.

Her chest falls on ragged breaths. She leans in close and brushes her lips along the side of my throat. Anastasia's muttering something over the line, but I don't hear it. "Drenched," Camilla breathes, her warm breath fanning over my neck.

I take a step back, and a small smile inches over Camilla's face. She scoots back on the sideboard and leans against the wall. Her robe parts, exposing her round breasts as she spreads her legs wide. My gaze falls to her bare pussy, and my entire body heats with want.

"Touch yourself," I say, my cock swelling with each second. Anastasia moans over the line as I watch Camilla's fingers tease over her clit then disappear inside her. She pulls her hand away, lifting her fingers to my mouth and sliding one over my bottom lip. I grab her wrist, slipping two of her fingers inside my mouth. She tastes like sin and power and every temptation I've ever wanted.

The phone drops to the floor, clattering over the hardwoods. I grip Camilla by the jaw and swallow hard. God, I want to fuck her. Ruin her. Make her hurt... I inch my way toward her mouth, my lips brushing hers, my hold on her jaw tightening. Her uneven breaths wash across my face. She's spread out in front of me. It would take nothing to throw her to the floor and fuck her. Blood rushes angrily through my body, begging me to claim her. My gaze falls to her parted legs, and I take a breath, placing my forehead against hers. "You're very brave, little kitty," I whisper before shoving her away.

I snatch the glass of brandy from the sideboard, and pick the phone up from the floor, disconnecting the call on my way back to the sofa. I make a point not to acknowledge Camilla when I grab the smoldering cigar from the ashtray and take a long puff, smoke swirling around my face. The news carries on, going over terrorist attacks, murders, all the things that instill fear within the public. And after a few moments, I catch Camilla's reflection on the TV screen as she walks behind the sofa. Her warm fingers skirt over the nape of my neck and goosebumps rush over my arm. There's a slight pause, as though she's waiting for me to react. And although my cock is straining against my pants, I stare at the screen, dismissing her with silence. She leaves the room and with her goes the crackling tension of a building fire. One I fear shall consume me eventually.

Chapter 15

Camilla

"Itch"- Nothing But Thieves

My heart pounds as I hurry back to my room, my pussy throbbing for that Russian prick. I can still feel his lips on my neck. Hear his deep voice commanding me to touch myself. And I did, because never is a woman weaker than when she is at the mercy of a powerful man. Yes, Ronan Cole is powerful in more ways than one.

I close my eyes and picture the way he walked through that room, people screaming, chaos ensuing all around him—*his* chaos. *His* assassination—and me at his side. He was drunk on the sheer havoc of it all, on the violence and the blood. It's that ruthless, effortless hold over someone's life that pulls me helplessly to him even as I wish to be free of him. I want to fuck him almost as much as I want to kill him... perhaps both at the same time? I bite my lip as I imagine riding Ronan, dragging a knife across his throat while he flashes that arrogant smile, no doubt laying waste to me as he bleeds out. I slam my bedroom door and press my back to it, inhaling several deep breaths. The sexual tension between us is so cloying, so all-consuming that, at times, it's hard to see through the thick fog he induces. I can never forget that he is the enemy because the second I do he will remind me of it.

A low buzz sounds somewhere in the room, and I narrow my eyes. There's nothing for a second, and then it sounds again. *Is that something... vibrating?* I walk around the room, listening before I stop in front of the dresser. *Buzz. Buzz.* I stare at the clutch I had at dinner. *Buzz. Buzz.* I snatch it from the dresser and glance inside before instantly snapping it shut. *Shit.* I throw the balcony doors open and step outside. The cold wind forces a violent shiver over my body as I check to make sure there are no cameras out here. I open the clutch, peer inside, and frown at the sight of the burner phone and charging cable tucked amongst my lipstick and compact. I think back to the party. My clutch was with me the whole time, but... Ronan was right next to me. He could have slipped it in here. *What if it's a test? Give me a phone and see what I do to betray him.*

Sighing, I take the phone out and flip it open to a find a blinking envelope in the corner of the screen. When I tap over it, a text message pops up: *The enemy of my enemy is my friend. I will be in touch soon. We will destroy Ronan Cole.* I close the phone and blow a breath through my lips.

Now, *is* this a trap set by Ronan? Maybe, but until this

mysterious *friend* makes it known what they want, I can't truly know. If it's a trap, well... All captives have a purpose: collateral. And collateral has an expiration date, at which point, said collateral gets a bullet. I ran a cartel; I know the drill. So, really, I have nothing to lose.

If this *friend* can help me fuck Ronan up, I'll die with a smile on my face.

Twenty-four hours.

I've been locked in this room for twenty-four hours with no word from Ronan. So much for his so-called freedom. Perhaps he's decided it's safer for him if I'm locked away.

I lie on my back, stroking my fingers over the expensive, satin sheets. I picture Ronan sucking the taste of my pussy from my fingers as he so desperately tried to cling to his rigid control. The bedroom door flies open, cracking against the wall, and I jump when Igor steps in holding another of those damn dress bags. "Boss wants you dressed in thirty minutes."

God, Ronan is such a dick. I snatch the dress bag from Igor, waiting for him to leave the room. I hate that I'm arm candy at Ronan's disposal, but I like the opportunity to make him weak in any way. Ronan Cole likes beautiful things and beauty is always a woman's strength. I've seen the want flickering in his eyes in those moments he's so close to losing control. And I want to watch him break, even if my own control is equally threatened. Dancing to his tune is my best shot of getting close, so I'll play his arm candy—for now.

I brush my hair and put on the dress, smoothing out the material before I glance in the mirror. The dress clings perfectly to my curves. The black lace tailored so delicately over the bright, crimson red satin does make quite the statement, and I must admit; he has good taste.

Taking one last look at my reflection, I grab my clutch and step into the hallway, swearing under my breath as I make my way to the top of the stairwell. From here, I can see Ronan standing by the door. The way his suit clings perfectly to him accentuates the look of power constantly oozing from him. When I reach the bottom step, he turns, his gaze lazily dragging over me. "You *are* so pretty in red." He smiles before checking his watch.

A servant opens the front door. *Dear god, can the man not open a door for himself?* —and we step into the frigid air and head to the waiting limo, the constant barrage of snow swirling around me. The door is opened for us and we climb in, the car promptly pulling away. Ronan's running his hand over his expensive suit, smug as ever when I glance at him. "So," I say, "Free roam of your house?"

His eyes gleam. "Does it make you angry when I lock you up?"

I feign a smile even though I want to stab him. "Oh, Russian, you haven't seen me angry." It's a lie. He's seen me plenty angry, but I don't like the bastard thinking he has power over me.

Curiosity flickers over his face.

Anger bubbles beneath my skin as I turn my gaze out the window. With Ronan, it's easy to forget what I'm doing. This back and forth is time consuming, and each time I seem to get close, he just pushes me back. I kill his enemies, then he locks me up. I partake in his little assassination, then he offers me some freedom. He watches me touch myself, and locks me up again. Round and round we go, getting caught in the danger and bloodlust of it all only for him to catch himself. There's a sense of impending catastrophe, like a clock just ticking away over my head. And Ronan Cole is the one holding it.

After a short drive, the limo pulls to a stop outside a gothic cathedral.

"Where are we?" I ask.

"The late Prime Minister's funeral." Ronan frowns, but I can tell he's fighting a grin. *Sick fuck*. "I do so enjoy a funeral." Now, he full on smiles.

"You know, even by my standards, this is warped." I glance through the window at the funeral attendees somberly filing to the front of the cathedral. "Pretty sure there's a special place in hell for people who attend a funeral to watch the sobbing family of the guy they had shot in the face... I'm still upset about that dress by the way."

"It was the back of the head," he says.

"Oh," I turn around, "so instead of the neat entry wound being in his face, he got his face blown off." I nod my head. "I didn't see, what with him being face down in a pool of blood. Closed casket it is then."

The slightest of grins tugs at his lips before the car door is, of course, opened for us. Ronan steps out, offering me his hand and pulling me from the car. Government security lines the black carpet leading to the steps of the cathedral. Beyond them, groups of photographers and press lift their cameras in the hopes of getting a shot of the funeral attendees. I drop my chin and school my expression into one I hope resembles grief. Ronan wraps his arm around my waist, his hand rubbing circles across my back as if he's consoling me. The irony is practically choking me.

He whisks us inside the cathedral, and the commotion from outside is replaced by a solemn organ tune echoing from the tall, stone ceiling. People greet Ronan and he respectfully nods at them as we make our way to the front of the church. We stop next to an empty row. I unfasten the buttons of the black fur coat I'm wearing, and Ronan slides the coat off my shoulders. I hear the slight gasp from the women sitting a row over. Of course, wearing a bright red dress to a funeral there's no way I could go unnoticed. Which I'm sure is exactly what he wanted. *He's such a bastard.*

He shrugs out of his coat and places his hand on the small of my back, guiding me into a pew and taking a seat.

His arm comes around my shoulders and he pulls me to his side. The distinct scent of his cologne and lingering cigar smoke surrounds me, and I find myself breathing it in as we settle into the seat. People whisper amongst themselves. Some make their way to the closed casket with heads hung and tissues dabbing at their eyes. I catch a blonde woman a few rows up glaring in my direction. It's the skinny blonde who was at Ronan's house, the one he got into the car with. I can't help the slight smirk that pulls at my lips. Ronan's fingers gently run through my hair, and her eyes burn with hatred. I know without a doubt that this woman wants Ronan more than her next breath. A man's arm wraps around her shoulders, and she blinks. He whispers something into her ear. She kisses his cheek, and so the plot thickens. I wouldn't expect anything less than for Ronan to chase a taken woman.

The funeral starts and it's every bit as boring as any funeral, only this time, I don't understand a word they're saying. I'm falling asleep, my head almost touching Ronan's shoulder when he clears his throat. "Do try to look like you aren't bored to death," he says.

I groan. "When does the drinking start?"

His eyes twinkle when he looks at me. "A man just died..." His face is so close I can practically taste the cigar smoke tinging his breath.

"So moral, Mr. Cole."

He hides his smile by pressing his lips to my forehead.

"Bad company ruins good morals."

I know this is all for public show, but still, my heartrate skitters a little. "That it does."

He trails a finger underneath my chin, lifting for me to look at him. His lips tip up as he skates his thumb across my bottom lip. "Get up."

I blink before looking around only to find the church empty. Several men have the coffin propped on their shoulders, looking impatiently at us. *How the hell did I not notice everyone leaving?* Ronan cocks a brow and stands, holding my coat out for me. I slip my arms through the sleeves, and take his arm as he leads me out of the church. The second we're outside, Ronan beelines straight for the blonde woman and the man standing beside her. She eyes me as we approach, her red lips pressing into a tight line.

"My condolences," Ronan says as he holds out a hand. The man glares at him. Cameras flash and he hesitantly takes Ronan's hand. "Such a shame," Ronan continues. "Even men of power aren't safe these days." There's a slight smirk to his lips, and I wonder...I drop my chin to my chest, trying to hide my grin. I'd be lying if I said I didn't enjoy these little power plays. I want to loathe the Russian, and I do to an extent, but I also respect him. The two emotions make for a volatile existence.

Ronan turns toward me, motioning with his hand. "President Derevichi, this is Camilla. A business associate of mine."

I flash the President my most charming smile and he grins, staring at me for just a beat too long. He stumbles forward a step, taking my hand and brushing his lips across my knuckles. "Camilla, call me Nikoli," he says. The blonde clears her throat and he releases my hand before he motions toward her. “And this is my wife, Anastasia.”

Oh, shit. Ronan's palm lands on my back. I work to keep the shock from my face as I turn to her. She paints a smile on her face, but I can see the hatred burning in her eyes. So, Ronan is fucking the President's wife. *Why?* I look her over. She's pretty in a somewhat regal way, but I know enough about Ronan to know this is too uncontrolled, too risky to be anything other than perfectly planned. Ronan’s hand glides to my hip and he pulls me tightly to his side. Her eyes flare. *So, he wants to make her jealous... and he's using me to do it.* Why does that annoy me? Not like I expected to be treated like anything other than one of his fucking pawns.

Ronan and Nikoli discuss something in quick-fire Russian. Nikoli seems agitated. Ronan is...well, Ronan. And Anastasia glares at me as though I’m the devil. I shoot a condescending grin back at her, half hoping she'll try and hit me. I'd snap her skinny ass like a twig.

"It was lovely to meet you, Camilla," Nikoli says, pulling my attention away from his whore of a wife.

"And you." I make a slow show of stepping close to him and kissing his cheek. "You do know your wife is fucking Cole?" I whisper, still smiling. He stiffens and I move back.

Nikoli's cheeks redden, his jaw tics. Oh, he's beyond enraged. My stomach flits with excitement. I can't explain the rush that comes with screwing up Ronan's perfectly crafted plans.

Ronan takes my arm and yanks me toward the street while Nikoli's security team whisk him and Anastasia to a waiting SUV. As soon as we're in the car, Ronan turns on me, his fingers wrapping possessively around my throat. His gaze bores into me as his free hand fumbles along the door pocket. I watch over his shoulder as he pulls a revolver. He cocks it and, without a word, presses it underneath my chin. I tilt my head back, staring into his unforgiving blue eyes as my heart leaps into a sprint. "You're going to shoot me?" I say, forcing my voice to remain level as I lift a brow.

"Should I not?" His lips twitch in a smile.

"Not like I have much say in the matter," I mumble. The cool barrel of the gun presses harder underneath my chin and I grit my teeth, refusing to break eye contact with him.

"Why did you tell him?"

I try to bite back my temper, I do, but it takes me by surprise, firing to the surface in a rush. "Because I fucking can. I'm not your lap dog to command and use and parade in front of your middle-aged whore, no matter how much you may think so." I exhale. "Maybe I just like fucking you in the ass, Russian. Any way I can."

There's a pause, a moment where his jaw sets.

Suddenly, a slow laugh rumbles from his chest. "You're more my lap dog than you think. I was hoping you would antagonize him, and you danced just like a puppet on my strings." He lowers the gun, sweeping a piece of hair from my face before he grabs the hem of my dress. He yanks it up my legs and shoves the gun between my thighs, staring at me. Waiting. Watching. My pulse thrums against my ears and a sweet adrenaline courses through my veins. Lust and rage swirl and blend together until I'm burning up, an inferno of want and hate in equal measure. I part my thighs and his lips tip up.

"Whatever shall I do with you, little kitty?" He slips the barrel underneath the lace of my underwear, trailing the cold metal over my pussy. I suck in a sharp breath and my hand flies to his jacket, my fingers gripping the material. He nudges the gun against me until it threatens to slip inside me. My heartbeat ratchets higher and higher, the pounding rhythm all I can hear. It's the danger, the thrill, the absolute knowledge of being on the very edge. One slip of his finger and this could end so very badly, but that's what makes it so exciting, so fucking intoxicating. This is what Ronan is, what he does. He owns fear, creates it and controls it until I'm left craving his brand of peril.

My free hand trails over his forearm, and I grab his wrist, pulling it toward me while rolling my hips. The barrel of the gun slides inside me, the cool metal meeting hot flesh. I bite my lip and tip my head back. A low growl rumbles through Ronan's chest and the sound of that tiny loss of control makes me hotter, wetter. This deadly dance—it's like nothing else. I may hate Ronan Cole, but he turns me on in ways that no man ever has or will. He has a power over me. We both know it, and yet I will deny it until the day he undoubtedly tires of me and puts a bullet in my head.

Chapter 16

Ronan

"Desperado" – Rihanna

The tip of the loaded gun disappears inside her. My pulse hammers in my chest. My cock begs for me to fuck her. Swallowing, I tear my gaze away from that breathtaking sight and look at her. Her head is tossed back, her eyes closed and her bottom lip is gripped between her teeth. She grinds against the gun still clutched in my hand as her legs fall farther apart. *So very naughty.*

I war with myself, my skin heating to an unbearable level. The primitive male in me screams to be freed, and he wins. Without hesitation, I pull the gun away, grab her by the throat, and shove her to the floorboard of the limo, settling between her spread thighs. The warmth of her pussy seeps through my slacks as I press against her. My fingers tighten around her throat, twitching as I skim my nose along the side of her neck. Sitting up, I trail the gun over her thigh, her side. Her throat is still in my grip when I move the gun along her cheek to those perfect red lips. She opens and sucks the wet barrel into her mouth with a slight moan.

"How does it taste?" I whisper, my finger leisurely resting on the trigger. My eyes drop to the scab on her chest, and I can't help but remember cutting her. Honestly, I'm barely able to restrain myself. This is foreplay. This is very hazardous foreplay. Things that anyone else would fear, she embraces, and it makes me drunk with lust and want and need. She's brimming with the most beautiful form of insanity, and I want to embrace it. I pull the tip of the gun from her mouth, watching as her tongue flicks over the open end of the barrel.

"I want you," I say, leaning by her ear. "But, I'm not going to touch you."

"I shouldn't want you," she whispers. And oh, how much those words sound like a desperate confession. *What to do? What to do?*

I shove away from her before sliding up onto the seat. "Touch yourself," I say, aiming the gun at her. I don't need to have her at gunpoint, she'll do it regardless, but the added element of danger makes it all the more exciting.

Her eyes flicker when she pulls the skirt of her dress around her waist. She slides her thong off, spreading her legs for me. The sight of such a volatile woman in such a vulnerable position makes my cock swell, and I'm certain she's enjoying this just as much as I am. Her hand dips between her legs and she slowly sweeps a finger over her clit on a moan. The man inside me wants nothing more than to defile her, but truly, reducing her to such a primal level of lust is so much better. She's spread out on the floor of a car on her way to a burial with her fingers inside herself, and all because I told her to do so. Because just as much as I want her, she very much wants me. And who is the sicker of the two? Captor or captive? Hunter or prey?

Her fingers sink knuckle deep, and she fucks herself hard, fast, angry. The sight of it drives me to the brink of losing complete control. A choked moan slips through her lips, and I can't stand it any longer. I keep the gun aimed at her while I yank at my belt and tug at my fly, fisting my cock when its finally freed. My hand slaps against my stomach as I force my pace to match hers.

The city creeps by outside as the motorcade winds through crowded Moscow. And here she and I are... like animals.

She moans, swearing under her breath while her back arches from the floor. The sweet chorus of her orgasm is all I need. Heat gathers in my stomach before spreading through my body in a violent show of force. My chin drops to my chest and I growl, coming hard and fast before I slump against the seat to catch my breath. *I lost control—to an extent*, I think as I fasten my belt. It's not until I notice the come stain on my Prada dress shirt that the annoyance sets in.

Camilla shoves her skirt back into place and pushes to her knees in front of me. I press the gun to her temple. Her hands land on my thighs as she leans over me and grazes her lips across my cheek. "You look so beautiful when you come," she whispers before moving to the seat next to me.

"What a dangerous game you play, little kitty,"

"Oh, but they're your games, Ronan. I just play." She pulls a compact from her bag and carefully applies a new layer of blood-red lipstick.

"You don't just *play*, Camilla."

"Now, now." She pats my arm. "Don't imply that you don't have absolute and complete control over my every action, Ronan."

My jaw tics and I turn to the window. Rows and rows of snow-covered tombstones and crosses pass by as we wind through the cemetery. Eventually, the limo slows and pulls to the side of the road. The driver hops out. The door opens and I grab Camilla's hand, dragging her to the edge of the seat as I step out.

People file out of the cars behind us, all making their way to the green tent set up on the hillside. I take Camilla's arm and loop it through mine just as Anastasia and Nikoli walk past. Anastasia's eyes lock on Camilla, and Camilla brings her lips to my ear. "I think she's obsessed. You know, women like that are liable to go crazy and murder you in your sleep." She kisses my cheek, all for show I know. But I like to be showy.

"She's more likely to murder *you*." I arch a brow, and she rolls her eyes.

We take a seat under the graveside canopy. Ana sits on the other side of the silver coffin, glaring at me, her leg anxiously bouncing. Her gaze shifts to my right and I glance at Camilla to find the two engaged in a possessive stare off. I lean in, sweeping the tendril of dark hair away from her ear. "Such a good little lapdog," I whisper before I kiss her neck.

"I told you already, I bite, Russian."

Forcing a look of remorse on my face, I stare straight ahead at the casket and wrap my arm around Camilla's shoulders. The minister steps behind the coffin and clears his throat, asking us to bow our heads. Camilla drops her chin to her chest, crossing herself. While everyone else prays, I watch Camilla, seemingly harmless with her head bowed in reverent prayer, but she is like a lotus flower. Pretty and deadly.

And I hate to admit it, but it is very much a thrill.

Chapter 17

Camilla

"Killing in the Name" – Rage Against the Machine

I slam my bedroom door shut. Fucking Russian! Every time I think I'm in control, he makes me unhinged.

He fucked me with a gun – a loaded gun— and I liked it. I wanted it! Hell, I can't remember ever being so turned on, so desperate for a man. Sex is *my* weapon, but he turns it on me so easily. I close my eyes, picturing the way he gripped his dick, the way his muscles strained and popped against his skin. The fierce yet utterly controlled look in his eyes as he watched me break apart on the floor of his limo.

My eyes snap open and I groan in frustration, flopping back on the bed. I'm supposed to be getting close to him the same way I got close to Jésus. The mantis does not fall into her own trap for fuck's sake. He's playing me every bit as hard as I'm playing him, but I have a lot more to lose. I need to break him. I need to make the devil weak.

I get up and go to the closet, shrugging a silk nightie over my head. It barely hits the top of my thigh, and as much as I don't care, I can't be too obvious. Ronan Cole is not one for obvious. So, I slip on a silk robe and tie it at my waist before leaving the room and walking down the stairs.

The low hum of a woman speaking in Russian floats through the foyer, and I follow the sound to the doorway of the front living room. There he sits, a glass of brandy in one hand and a cigar in the other. I walk into the room and move straight past him, over to the drink cabinet in the corner. His eyes burn a hole in my back as I pour a drink, and I stare at the wooden sideboard where only days ago I sat and touched myself for him. I smirk at his uptight control. *He won't touch me? We'll see about that.* I want to pluck his dirty secrets out one by one and use them against him.

When I turn around, his eyes are fixed on the TV. "What havoc have you caused today?" I jokingly ask.

"I wouldn't call burying the Prime Minister havoc, per se."

I cross the room and take a seat on the sofa a couple of feet away from him, crossing my legs. "You know, going to the funeral of a man you killed has to be bad juju." I tip the drink back, swallowing it in one gulp.

His gaze strays from the glass in my hand to the bottle on the sideboard. "That's my special brandy you're so carelessly necking..."

I roll my eyes. "If you're going to drink, then drink.

Don't sip it like a pussy."

"Fine brandy is meant to be savored."

"Sure." I push to my feet and go back to the sideboard, picking up the crystal decanter of his precious brandy. I take the top off and walk back to the sofa, pouring a splash into my glass.

He eyes me before snatching the decanter from my grasp. "You may very well be the closest thing to a savage I've ever stumbled across."

"Oh, Russian," I laugh. "Don't pretend you don't like things a little wild." With a smug smile, I lift my glass and down the contents, my eyes never leaving his. "Live a little," I say.

He motions toward the television and smooths his hand down the front of his jacket. "I do live a little."

I glance at the TV. I don't understand what they're saying, but images of a factory with Chinese writing and missiles scroll across the screen. "I heard you were into weapons." I narrow my eyes. "Risky business."

His eyes flash with delight. "I like their power. The fear they instill."

"Uh-huh. I prefer not to attract the attention of every government agency in the world. I bet the Americans have a massive hard-on for you— a Russian arms dealer." I have to laugh.

"The FBI and I are like this," he crosses his fingers together on a smile.

He's joking, right? His eyes hold mine. *Jesus fuck, I don't think he is.* "Just..." I point at him and shake my head. "I need a drink." I move to snatch the brandy bottle and he simply grabs my throat, holding me at arm's length.

"No more of my celebratory brandy." He nods back to the sideboard. "Have all the Russian vodka you like."

I make a face. "What do you think I am? Russian? Who the hell drinks vodka?" I say, getting up. I go over to the cabinet, open the decanter, and sniff it. "God, it smells like gasoline." I pour some into my glass and neck it, wincing.

He shakes his head. "Do you intend to get yourself drunk?"

"I'm stuck here with your charming company in Dracula's fucking castle. What do you think?" I patronize as I pour another glass.

He drags a hand down his face before pushing up from the couch and stalking toward me. He takes the vodka, pours another drink, then corks the bottle. "You can't be hungover tomorrow."

"Why?" I sigh. "Are you planning another assassination?"

"I have a ribbon cutting ceremony at the Children's Hospital." he grins. "The new Ronan Cole Bone Marrow Transplant unit is opening.

I stare blankly at him. "Now you *are* joking..." I tip my head back and release a breath. "Fuck, I can't even tell."

"I think a blue dress would work nicely for tomorrow."

"Do I have a choice in this? Charity and saintly behavior...really not my thing."

A soft laugh slips through his lips. "For you, there is no such thing as a choice any longer." His finger swipes my cheek.

"Pluh-uh-ease." He scowls at me. "Repeat," I say. "Pleeaase." More scowling. I can't help but grin. His jaw ticks and I find it sexier than I'd like.

"The amusement you provide is quickly wearing off."

I shrug. "I'd say the same, but you are the least amusing person I've ever met." I know I push him. I'm not sure if I just like the thrill, the sense of danger, or I want to see if I can make him snap and kill me. He says I'm only alive for his amusement, but we both know that's not true. There's more to it. I drag my eyes over his expensive suit. Maybe he's just like all the others. Perhaps he just wants to fuck me. "Why do you need me to go?" I ask.

"Because a man such as myself does not show up alone, and your beauty looks good on me." He swipes his special brandy from the sideboard.

"Well, I'm so glad I make the cut for your ever-growing harem." I tilt my head. "Right next to the Russian President's wife." I place my hand on my chest. "My daddy would be so proud."

A slight smirk tugs at his lips. "Be ready by ten," he says, turning his back to me. I'm dismissed.

I stand on a raised platform overlooking a crowd of standard, white-collar people. Board member types and doctors huddle close to the stage, smiling at Ronan. *If only they knew...* He gives some speech in Russian and they applaud him. He turns a wide grin on me and cameras flash. I fake a smile, watching as he snips a pale blue ribbon with a pair of gold scissors. People clap some more, and Ronan shakes a few hands before moving over to me and placing a hand on my waist as his lips brush over my cheek. "Smile, Krasivaya." He turns toward the crowd as the cameras continue to snap photos.

I feign a moment of coyness and turn my face slightly into his chest. "My fucking face hurts, Russian."

"Ah, but the pictures will look so pretty in the newspapers. People may even think you're a civilized woman."

I continue to smile through gritted teeth. "And people will think you're the second coming of Mother Theresa, and not the guy who probably plotted her death for unknown purposes."

He glances at me and grins. "I liked Mother Theresa."

"I knew it." I narrow my eyes at him. "I *knew* she was corrupt. No one is that damn righteous."

He laughs as he places a possessive hand on my waist and guides me off the stage. People stop him left and right, shaking his hand and singing his praises, until finally, we make it outside. The car is waiting in the roundabout, his driver holding the door. I climb in and Ronan slides in beside me, still smiling at people gathering outside as the door closes. The car pulls away and he leans his head back against the seat on an exhale.

"How do you do this?" I groan. "All the smiles and the bullshit and the fucking niceties."

"I rather enjoy the theatrics of it. The manipulation of painting one face over another and another until I'm seen as nothing but a saint, or the devil depending on who you ask."

I snort. "You're not that good, Ronan. The devil can't hide his horns."

"The devil doesn't have horns, little kitty."

"No, apparently, he wears a custom suit."

His eyes gleam. "You may very well be the most entertaining hostage I've ever had. Congratulations!"

I plaster a sweet smile on my face. "You're a dick, you know that?" He, of course, ignores me.

The city passes by the window and I wonder how long he'll keep me. How much longer I have to figure out a way to destroy him. We drive across town, and the car slows to a stop in front of a restaurant with groups of businessmen loitering outside.

The driver opens the door and we both step out, heading toward the restaurant. A young hostess greets us at the door with a tense smile. Without a word, she guides us to a private room at the back of the building. Ronan stops in the doorway and shakes his head, saying something in Russian to her. She goes rigid and pales before she turns on her heel, leading us into the main restaurant. He literally puts the fear of god into people, and I won't pretend it's not entertaining to watch.

The hostess sets the menus on a table by the window. Ronan pulls my chair out and the hostess stares at me, dumbfounded. I guess he doesn’t often take women to lunch... He says something to the hostess, and she hurries away. Frowning, I take my seat and he pushes the chair in before sitting across from me. He lays his napkin across his lap and flashes a blinding smile at me. My stomach tightens slightly in response. Fuck him and his model-worthy face.

"Why are we here? Are you meeting someone?" I ask, but there are only two chairs.

He glances at his watch. "It's noon.”

"And? You don't make passive aggressive threats before five?"

"It's lunchtime." He pauses. "We're eating lunch."

I wrinkle my nose. "We're eating lunch....in a restaurant...like a date?"

A large grin shapes his lips. "Precisely."

I lean back in my chair and drum my nails over the crisp, white tablecloth. "Let me guess, the President and his wife are due here any minute?"

"No."

What the hell is he up to now? He's always up to

something. I don't mind being a part of his schemes if I know what they are, or at least vaguely know what they are, but I don't like not knowing someone's motivations. Humming to himself, he picks up his menu, and I turn my attention to the one in front of me. It's all in fucking hieroglyphics.

A waitress comes over with a bottle of wine and she pours two glasses. Ronan closes his menu and folds his hands on the table in front of him as he talks to her, I guess ordering. I jab my finger against a random item on the menu and show the waitress. She doesn't acknowledge me.

"I ordered for you," he says as the waitress takes the menus and disappears.

I roll my eyes. "Of course you did."

He reaches across the table and takes my hand in his. "So, dear Camilla, what is the worst thing that's ever happened to you?" I glare at him and attempt to pull my hand away, but his grip becomes painful. "Leave your hand," he orders.

"None of your business," I narrow my eyes at him, "Russian."

He moves his hand away from mine. "I guess it would be a sore subject for you, that not even your own father would rescue you. The humanity of darkness can be awfully hard to swallow." *How does he know everything?*

"My father was a business man." I jerk my chin up. "I'm not a damsel, Russian. I don't need rescuing. After all, the darkness is what makes people like you and I, is it not?"

"It is." He pulls a cigar from his jacket and lights it. "I find the darkness," he takes a long drag, "rather titillating."

"What about your father, Ronan? How did he die?" If he wants to poke me then I'll poke him.

There's a slight flicker in his eyes like a match being struck and the faintest of smiles curls his lip. "He was brutally murdered." His finger trails across his neck mimicking a knife cut. "His throat slit from ear to ear."

I take a sip of wine, watching him carefully. "I do hope you found the man who did it."

"Oh... I did." He picks up the knife from the table, sliding his fingers along its edge. "The thing about power, Camilla, it can only be managed by very bad men, and my father only *thought* he was a bad man. He had too much..." he stabs the knife into the table and I jump, "heart."

"You killed him?" I breathe, surprised by the wave of pity that washes over me. My father was bad in every sense of the word, but I loved him, respected him. Ronan's world is reduced to strength versus weakness. The powerful versus the powerless. I'm in awe of it, but it's tragic in a way.

"It was only business." A sadistic grin spreads over his lips, and I can see that, to him, it's exactly that. He studies me, those cold, blue eyes boring into me as though to pluck me apart bit by bit. "People like you and I, we rise out of ashes," he says. "It's when a man is at his lowest that he finds the drive to become great, is it not?"

"My father used to say that a man must be face down in the dirt before he truly finds himself. He'll either lie there, or he'll find a will the likes of which he's never known." I know from firsthand experience just how true that statement is. "But I cannot imagine that you were ever kissing the dirt, Russian."

He puffs on his cigar again. "I did come from very *humble* beginnings. But you did not."

I eye his expensive suit. I know what he's doing—he wants to know things about me because knowledge is power. I want to shut it down, but I also need to know about him, so I offer a tentative trade. Inhaling as his eyes hold me prisoner, I quirk my lips up. "No. Drugs and blood pay well. My father ran it all, started it all, back when cocaine hadn't even touched American soil." I shrug and trail my finger around the bottom of my wine glass.

"How proud he would be to know his daughter ran the Juarez cartel as opposed to his only living son."

"Gabriel didn't have the stomach to do what needed to be done in the early days," I say carefully.

"Seems he still doesn't have the stomach."

"Perhaps." I glance at Ronan. "Or perhaps you underestimate him."

"Come now, Camilla." A knowing smile crosses his lips as he raises his cigar.

"Gabriel is... eccentric at times."

"I don't wish to talk about your brother or *my* cartel,"

he says. “Only you."

I sigh and tap my nail over the table top. "What would you like to know about me?" I say through clenched teeth, my patience rapidly fading.

"Why fire?"

I narrow my eyes. "Why not fire?"

"I did not miss it when you said there was something spiritual about it, Krasivaya. And I do not tolerate lies well."

"I didn't lie," I say. He lifts a brow. Waiting.

Releasing a long breath, I tip my head forward for a moment and allow the memories I try to keep buried to surface. "The first time I was taken by my father's enemies,” I say, “I was fourteen. Innocent. Naive. And you're right, he didn't come for me. They raped me, tortured me, and burned me..." I smile sarcastically. "It did something to me. Destroyed me, but as you say; I rose from the ashes stronger, cleansed if you will. I didn't *need* my father to save me. I escaped and burned that house to the ground with my captors inside, so yes, it's powerful and spiritual."

"I see." He puffs on his cigar, his eyes dancing with a sick understanding before he falls quiet.

The waitress comes out of nowhere and places our plates on the table, and we eat in silence, the classical music drifting through the restaurant providing an ironic theme tune to our lunch date. After a few minutes, I place my knife and fork on my half-eaten plate of food. "Why the cartel?” I say. “We both know you don't need anyone's help." This question has been eating away at me since he took me. The cartel is powerful but Ronan Cole is playing a different game entirely. It doesn't make any sense, and yet I know enough to understand that Ronan does nothing without reason. I narrow my eyes and take another sip of wine. "Jésus told me about the land that 'the Russian' tried to buy..."

He dabs at his mouth with his napkin. "I thought it would make a nice spot for a vacation home, what with that beautiful lake and the buzzing insects." He grins.

That little thrill zips through my chest, the rush of having caught an opponent unaware. "I'm sure. Clearly you crave a warmer climate." I've never seen anyone look more at home in this frozen wasteland than this bastard. There's something there, in that lake. Something he needs enough to slaughter an entire cartel for. Ronan takes a bite of steak, and the rest of lunch is carried out without another word.

The waitress drops off the check. Ronan tosses a stack of Rubles on the table, pushes to his feet, and leaves with barely a glance my way. I follow him to the front of the restaurant, because, what else am I going to do? The icy air whips around me as soon as I step outside. I tilt my chin to my chest in an effort to keep warm, and walk into something solid. Ronan whirls around and catches me in his arms. I go tense for a second. He beams before pulling his arm tightly across the small of my back. His lips brush my cheek, his warm breath blowing over my cold skin. I feel like I'm getting whiplash from his hot and cold emotions.

"I've never tasted a pussy as sweet as yours," he whispers against my throat. "And the way your cheeks flush when you come...*divine*."

My heart bangs in my chest as I slowly lift my gaze. His blue eyes pin me to the spot as his fingertips run across my cheek. "What are you doing?" I ask, confused.

He answers with a smirk that is pure sin, then he leans in until his lips are only a breath away from mine. "Smile for the camera, little kitty." *Camera? God, he's an ass.* I shove at his chest, but he refuses to let me go. "Let's not fight," he tuts.

"Fuck you, Russian!" I manage to get away from him and storm to the car, but he's right behind me, laughing. The driver hurries to my side and opens the door. I climb in followed by Ronan, and the door slams shut. "You know," I sat, "I don't mind being used, but a little fucking warning before you assault me in the street would be nice." An angry exhale rushes from my lungs, but of course, he doesn't acknowledge me.

I want to get close. I need him to want me. *Genuinely* want me. We're both wrapped in schemes on top of schemes. Him using me, me using him. There are no lines here, only inky, black smudges masquerading as some form of civilized warfare.

So it seems there is no honor to be had, only dirty tactics.

Chapter 18

Ronan

"No Retreat" – Joe Marson

The morning sun dances over my desk as I sit, watching the security footage of Camilla sleeping. I do rather enjoy being able to spy on her like this... She's been tossing and turning. Thrashing. I lean back in my chair, curious about what she's dreaming. A slight thrill shoots through me when she sits bolt upright in the bed, her chest rising in ragged swells. I can only hope I'm the monster in her nightmares, it would be such an honor.

A servant steps into the room and I close the screen. I watch him as he crosses the room, but his eyes remain trained on the floor. Without a word, he places the tray with my morning paper and coffee at the end of my desk and leaves. I immediately flip to the business section, smiling when my eyes land on the lovely picture of Camilla and I outside the restaurant, my lips against her delicate throat. There's a slight blush to her cheeks which I find grave satisfaction in. Above the photo is the header: *Is Business*

Mogul Ronan Cole Still Russia's Most Eligible Bachelor?

I laugh. If only those women knew what truly lurks beneath... My phone rings on my desk, and I groan when I see Anastasia's name flash on the screen. Exhaling, I accept the call and can hear Anastasia screaming before I pull the phone to my ear. "Yes?"

"Why would you, Ronan?" Ana shouts between sobs. "How long have you been seeing her?"

I find it amusing that the woman who was having an affair can point fingers. "Not long," I say. Another wretched sob crosses the line. "You can't possibly be angry at me. You're married, Ana. Married! And your husband knows about us."

"But I love you."

"And what am I to do? Sit and wait for you? You can't leave him. He'll never allow you to leave, I'm just trying to—"

"Have you slept with her?"

My stomach flutters with excitement. "Ana..."

"Have you fucked her?"

"I'm just trying to get over you. My heart's broken, Ana, it truly is because I can never really have you." *Lies. All such pretty, pretty lies.* "I can't do this anymore," I say, and hang up. Love is a pathetic emotion too many people allow to rule them.

Smiling, I pick my phone up and dial Igor. It rings once.

"Yes, boss?" he says.

"When will the plane be ready for China?"

"Two hours."

"Very good. Lock the little kitty up, while I'm gone, would you?"

"Gladly," he says, and I hang up.

The phone buzzes again, Ana's name flashing on the screen. I shut the ringer off, drumming my fingers over the table as I contemplate what truly rules the world, money or love. After all, love is what many wars have been fought for, and pretending it's an emotion I'm capable of is how I've started many wars myself. It may be how I start this one...

A small Chinese man buzzes Donovan and I through a set of metal doors. We follow a long hallway to another set of doors. An alarm beeps, the doors swing open to a dark room and the smell of gunpowder wafts out. The lights flicker on, and I inhale a deep breath, beaming. The room is filled to the brim with boxes of ammunition. "So good to see the supply from Mexico has been steady," I say.

We're lead to another room, and the man types in a passcode before the lock clicks. The door opens and a cloud of cold fog billows through the doorway as we step inside. The chill to the air rouses me, and then my eyes lock on three small, glass boxes placed on the middle of a table. Inside each box is a silver torpedo no bigger than a laptop. My heart palpitates, the excitement teems through my blood like a lethal dose of heroin.

Another man in a white lab coat enters the room, clearing his throat as he holds out his hand to me. "I'm Chen Hsu. It's very nice to meet you, Mr. Cole." I shake his hand, my eyes still glued to the shiny objects. Honestly, I can barely contain myself. "Each bomb," he says, "has an impact of one-hundred fifty megatons. Twice that of the largest nuclear weapon ever detonated. The Devil's Dust you've been mining has proven very powerful." He beams, pleased with himself.

"Wonderful," I say, stepping to the edge of the table. The man shifts uncomfortably and I glance up.

"They are very delicate," he says.

I swipe a finger over the edge of the smooth glass with a grin. "Even better. I can't wait to watch the test detonation; it should be so festive." Donovan chuckles beside me. "You are the scientist responsible for the development, correct?"

The man nods.

"And no one else has access to that formula, correct?" I ask, lifting a brow.

"No one, as you requested."

"Very good. I'll need the files, proprietary information and such, in the event something dreadful were to happen to you." I smile and he shifts uneasily on his feet, his gaze drifting from me to Donovan and back. "Well then, shall we prepare for the premier?" I say with a clap of my hands.

Exhaling, Chen nods and motions toward the door. We step back into the hallway. My face is flush with anticipation, and I'll not lie, there's a little pep in my step.

"You're rather jovial," Donovan says.

"Of course, it's the day I've been waiting on for seven years."

We follow Chen through the narrow corridor, passing team after team of men in lab coats. Finally, we're lead into a breakroom. A large, plasma television with a live picture of a barren desert and blue sky hangs on the far wall.

I take a seat at the table, folding my hands on my lap as I stare at the screen. "Jung-Hwa is aware that his country is about to blow a crater in the Gobi Desert as a show of power to the Chinese?" I speak in Russian to Donovan so the little scientist won't understand me.

Donavan nods. A fissure of delight tears through me. Pawn by pawn, I've placed men—very corrupt men— in seats of power with the promise of money. Anton, Jung-Hwa, soon the American President... It's all working like an orchestrated symphony, and I'm the master conductor. After all, it takes a lot to construct a fake war. "Oh, " I say, "and how angry everyone will become. Nuclear warheads are so taboo these days."

A phone in the room rings and the man answers it, shouting in Chinese before slamming it back down. He points at the screen and I watch, my stomach absolutely swimming with butterflies. Suddenly, a bright light washes out the screen. There's a loud boom and seconds later the floor to the building we're in rattles. My cheeks hurt from smiling. Adrenaline rumbles through my entire body as I anxiously watch the static fizzle on the screen. Within a few seconds, a pixelated image blips onto the monitor before slowly coming into focus, showcasing an aerial view of the blast site. My chest tightens and I push up from my seat, knocking the chair over as I step toward the television. Through the cloud of ash and smoke I can make out the blackened earth. Land passes underneath the drone, but it's all scorched. All demolished. Miles and miles of destruction. This is a weapon all the major power players will want when they find out their enemy is in possession of it. Because I'll make sure the enemies have one... I glance at Chen. "Where do you keep your files?"

"Locked in my office."

Donovan stands and I adjust my cufflinks as he approaches the little scientist. He grabs his shoulders and spins him around, quickly jabbing a blade into his jugular. The man grabs at his neck, gasping for breath as the blood spurts through his fingers. He buckles and his knees hit the floor with a thud before he falls face first onto the tile. "What a shame to snuff out such genius, but..." I take a breath, "you never can be too careful with your secrets."

Donovan wipes the blade of the knife clean with a handkerchief and we step toward the door. "Grab those files from his office," I say, taking one last look at the glorious image on the screen.

Chapter 19

Camilla

"Trouble" – The New Respect

Ronan has been gone for two days. And for two days, I've been locked in this damn room!

I pace the room like a caged animal, crawling out of my skin. I have to talk to Gabriel, and that's not happening while Ronan is here. I debated using the burner phone I've hidden in the toilet tank, but I still can't be sure it's not actually Ronan. I need to get out and get to another phone. Now. While he's not here. He said himself his men have orders not to kill me. Funny, I can get past the ones with the guns, yet the unarmed man in the suit stops me in my tracks.

There's a knock on the door. The lock clicks, and I watch as one of Ronan's men brings a tray into the room. He flashes a nervous glance in my direction, and I sit on the edge of the bed. Smiling, I cross one leg over the other, and my dress rides up my thigh. His eyes drop to my legs before he quickly looks away. I've been here long enough to learn all the men that come in and out of here. This one is young, inexperienced. The weak link. You'd think after my little bonfire they'd be more careful about who they send in here.

He turns his back on me as he places the tray on the bedside table—like I said, inexperienced. I quickly stand and tiptoe over to him. My footfalls are muted by the thick carpet, so I'm surprised when he whips around, his body tense. I flick my hair over my shoulder as I reach out and trail my finger down the center of his chest. He glances at my hand working down to the waist of his slacks. His breaths come in short bursts, his eyes close—that's a mistake. I jab him in the throat with two fingers and knee him between his legs. He buckles to the floor, gasping for breath. He's so young. I almost feel bad when I move behind him and wrap my arm around his neck. He chokes and wheezes as I grip the top of his head and violently twist. The satisfying crunch of bone is followed by silence, and he falls face down on the carpet. Yes, guilt is occasionally a factor, but so is the fact that you should beware of the company you keep. Working with men like Ronan Cole will get you killed.

I glance at that fucking camera in the corner of the room. I don't know how much time I have, so I check him for weapons. No gun, but he does have a knife.

I grab a knee length fur coat from the closet and pull on a pair of boots. My heart hammers in my chest. The last time I got out was because I was pissed and I wanted to annoy Ronan. This is different. I don't want to start a blood bath; I just need to get out. The door creaks as I slowly open it, and I peek down the hallway. It’s empty, so I hurry out and make my way through the house, slinking along the walls and making sure to avoid the areas with cameras. The front is heavily guarded since my last escape. And while the vehicles are easy to get to, I'd be fighting off an army once I got in one. The back is the best option.

I hurry along the hallway, stopping at the elevator and pressing the down arrow before I hide behind the corner. My palm slicks with sweat as I clutch the knife in my hand. I think I’ve avoided the cameras until now, but they'll see the body in my room... There's a ping and I hear the doors slide open. I wait, listening for someone to step off, but there’s only silence. I pop around the corner and slip into the corner of the elevator. There’s a beep with each floor I pass, and when the doors open, I’m in a basement. Steel garage doors line the far wall and rows of luxury cars sit in each bay. *The Russian really does have too much money.*

Glancing around, I spot a key box on the wall and I go to it, managing to force open the lock with the tip of the knife. My pulse bangs in my ear as I snatch a key and press the unlock button. Headlights on a bright red Jaguar flash as a soft chirp echoes around the garage, and I hurry to it. It's not exactly inconspicuous, but at least it’s fast. I climb in, start the engine, and glance around for a garage remote. *Fuck, there isn't one.* There’s a sharp pinging noise followed by another. Bullets ricochet off the cars around me. I press the gas and the engine rumbles, snarling like an angry beast.

"I'm sorry," I say, and slam it into drive. The car shoots forward and I brace, closing my eyes as it collides with the garage door. The windshield cracks and bows, but it doesn't break. The garage door hinges screech in protest as they begin to tear from the runners. I press all the way down on the accelerator, tires spinning, engine revving. As soon as the mangled doors scrape over the roof of the car, I floor it. The car drifts, skidding around the back of the house before I speed up the drive. Guns fire as I approach the guard house, but the men aren't aiming at me. *Ronan and his no kill orders.* I crash through the front gate, snow flying everywhere as the metal entrance rips off its hinges.

I glance in the rearview. A string of SUVs barrel up the drive after me. I slam my foot down on the gas, and they fall behind. *Shouldn't be hard to hard to outrun them.* After a few sharp turns, I lose them. I drive for about an hour, and when I feel it's safe, I pull up to a gas station. The pumps are rusted and the advertisements in the ice-covered windows are faded. I don't bother to cut the engine before I open the door and run to the shop. The bell to the door tinkles and I stop in the doorway, looking around the messy store. My breath fogs in front of my face. *No heat.* Someone coughs and I turn toward the sound, stepping around the shelving. There's an old man bundled in a thick coat, toboggan, and gloves sitting behind a counter. He looks up at me with tired eyes.

"Phone?" I ask. He frowns at me. *Damn it.* Spanish and English are all I know. I hold my hand to my ear in the universal phone sign, and he nods before waving me behind the counter. He points to the floor, at an old phone. I pick it up and dial Gabe's number. The phone rings several times and I swear under my breath. I only have so much time to do this before Ronan finds me, because he absolutely *will* find me.

Finally, Gabe picks up. "Hola."

"Gabe!"

He pauses for a second. "Where is that fucking Russian?"

"Not here, but it won't be long. I cannot *believe* you sold out to him." I sigh. Not important right now. "Look, I need you to listen. The land, with the lake...that's why he wants us. There's something there. He tried to buy it off Jésus. Funny that he then suddenly makes a deal with you to take Jésus out... Find it and use whatever it is he wants so badly to get us out from under that Russian fuck."

"What land? There are a million lakes in fucking Mexico!"

"Estrallado Largo."

"What the fuck does he want with a meteor site? Ai, ai, ai. He's fucking loco. I swear to god, when I get out from under him, I'm going to shove his pale dick up his asshole."

"I don't know. I didn't get a chance to ask him what his master plan to take over the world is. Fuck! Just do it."

"You find a way out."

"Gabe," I sigh. "I'm not sure I'll make it out of this one." There's a pause. "You should have just let him kill me, Gabriel. You've shown him a weakness, and now he'll push the advantage. Papa taught you better."

"I'm not letting the Russian fuck kill you, Camilla."

I'd tell Ronan a thousand times that I would sacrifice Gabriel for my cartel. It's what our father taught us to do, to never negotiate and show weakness. The truth is, sometimes sentiment is all we have. I love Gabriel. He's the only person I have left, and I know all too well that this world can be very lonely.

"I have to go," I whisper. "I love you." I never say it, but I don't know when or if I'll ever get the chance again. I don't wait for a response; I just hang up. The old man stares at me for a second and I stand up, smiling at him in thanks. I've done what I needed to do, now I just have to wait for Ronan's men to find me, which shouldn't take long. I climb back inside the battered Jaguar and head for Moscow. Might as well make a day of it.

Chapter 20

Ronan

"Living Dead Girl" – Rob Zombie

I step off the plane, parting ways with Donovan as I head toward the waiting car. Igor stands next to the open door with a solemn look on his face.

"She got out," he says as I bend to slide into the car.

"I'm sorry?"

The door slams shut and the car pulls off. "Camilla got out."

"You say that as though she's nothing but a stray dog." I groan. "How difficult is it to keep one woman locked in a room? How many men did she kill this time?" It shouldn't excite me, to think of the anger swirling in her eyes as she goes on a killing rampage, but it does.

"One, and she stole a car."

"Of course she did."

"We have the GPS coordinates. She's in Moscow."

"And... why is no one after her?" I just had the most spiritual moment of my life with that nuclear weapon only to have it tainted by a level of incompetency I cannot understand.

He shifts in the seat. "We thought it would be best if you handled her."

I pull my phone from my pocket and pull up the GPS. The little red dot blips right outside The Kremlin. Of course, she's not hiding. She knows better.

Half an hour later, the car pulls into a crowded parking lot. Through the window I can see my Jaguar. The hood is smashed, sides dented, and a lovely array of bullet holes decorate the back. Now *that* makes me angry.

Before the driver has a chance to climb out, I throw open the door and step into the frigid wind. Igor opens his door, and I hold up a finger, halting him. "Stay here, Igor," I say as I pull my coat together and head down the snow laced sidewalk. I round the corner, stepping between a group of women, and there Camilla stands at the gate of the Kremlin, dressed in a fur coat with her back to the street. *She did this just to defy me. To get a rise.* My jaw tics, and I close my eyes. She craves my anger, so she shall not have it. "Have you had enough sightseeing and murder for the day?" I ask, stepping up behind her.

She glances over her shoulder, and a sheet of dark hair falls over one side of her face. "It was one guy. I just wanted to see Moscow. I don't appreciate being locked up like a rebelling child."

I study her face. The flicker of fearlessness that dances

within her eyes gives me a rise I rather enjoy, but this defiance... It gives me much more than a rise, and I need to snuff this out immediately. I grab her firmly by the elbow, and walk, pulling her behind me as I head toward the car. Igor is waiting with the door open, and I shove Camilla inside. I climb in followed by Igor, and as the car pulls away she points through the window, smiling.

"Sorry about your Jaguar," she says. "It was a nice car."

I pull a cigar from my jacket and light it, staring at her as the smoke streams in front of my face.

She holds up her hands. "Just take it out of Gabe's cut of...whatever."

My blood pressure steadily ticks up notch by notch. She doesn't know when to keep her mouth shut, and there's a fine line between entertainment and annoyance. Part of me wishes for nothing more than to teach her what true fear means, for me to go back to my roots and soak my hands in blood; then part of me wants to fuck her while I choke her, taking her to the very brink of death while I'm buried deep inside her. How this all plays out in the end will be a surprise to us both, that I'm certain of.

I glance at Igor. "She says I treat her like a rebellious child," I say, smirking as I look at Camilla. "She doesn't appreciate how kind I've been with providing her with such lavish accommodations, so maybe she'll appreciate if I treat her like the hostage she truly is." I stroke my finger over her cheek. "I will miss looking at your pretty face though."

She knows she's in trouble, yet she holds her head high. She does wear that arrogance like a crown. Oh, what fun she'll have in the cold basement with all those other poor souls. I'd be lying if the thought of her suffering didn't utterly delight me. I'm sick, possibly even horrible, but what good man would ever be in my position? I'd take power over morals any day.

It's been two days since Camilla was taken into the old bomb shelter underneath this house. Two days of quiet. I sit with my brandy and cigar in hand, watching the news. So it seems the Gobi Desert was bombed by one of China's enemies a few days ago. How terribly awful. *What is this world coming to?* I find myself smiling.

My attention is drawn away from the carnage when the door to the living room creaks open. Igor steps into the room, his cheeks flushed, and a phone pressed to his ear. "Kill them," he says before hanging up.

"What's happened now?" I ask, taking a sip of brandy.

"The last shipment of Devil's Dust was stolen."

My teeth grind together, tension building in my neck. "Did you track it? Where is it?"

"At one of Estrada's safe houses."

I laugh. Of course it is. Funny that only two days after his sister escaped, a shipment of presumably useless powder goes missing *and* ends up at her stupid brother's house. Anger heats my blood, coiling around me as I stare through Igor. "Did you have someone detain him?"

"Yes, boss."

I swallow hard before pushing to my feet and smoothing the wrinkles out of my shirt. "I'm going down to pay her a visit." I'm barely able to restrain my voice. Her complete disregard for her own life thrills me to no end. Camilla is the very definition of reckless. She has no control, and that is like an aphrodisiac to me, because when there is no fear, no concern for one's self, the possibilities of what I could do to her are infinitely endless.

Chapter 21

Camilla

"Bad Habits" – The Kooks

Emergency lights flicker overhead before they completely black out. One by one, they hum back to life, lighting up all the way to the end of the basement. This is more of a bomb shelter I suppose, filled with beds and at least twenty people. I sit with my back against the cold wall and my legs stretched out on a rickety cot that's bolted to the floor, watching each of them. Wondering what they did to land on Ronan Cole's shit list.

I bet they didn't trash his car, kill his men, and escape.

A shiver works through me and I gather the scratchy, wool blanket around me. It irritates my skin, but I still smile, because I got a reaction. Ronan handled it the only way he could—by removing me from his presence. I only hope that Gabriel manages to find something, because honestly, I don't know how much longer I can go toe to toe with that man before I snap. I want to kill him, I want to hurt him, I want to end everything that he is and has, but... That raw authority he commands so effortlessly— it's like a magnet to someone like me. He may well be the only man to truly challenge me, and that's a one in a million shot. I watch the way he owns everyone, and I crave his ownership every bit as much as I loathe it. I'm not a woman who believes in love or even lust, but wild animal magnetism... that *is* Ronan Cole. There's nothing rational or fucking sensible about it, just pure, unadulterated primal need. I want to conquer the alpha male. Simple.

The click of the bolt sliding away from the door catches my attention. The hinges creak as the door slowly opens. Light spills through the doorway, silhouetting the suited form of the devil himself. Ronan snaps his fingers and two men walk into the room, approaching me and grabbing both my arms. I'm forced to my feet, and they walk me to the door, stopping right in front of Ronan. He stares down at me, those cold and completely unforgiving blue eyes locking with mine.

"Ronan." I tilt my head to the side and flick my tangled hair over my shoulder.

His jaw clenches and a muscle ticks before he turns and walks away. The men shove through the doorway, the door slamming shut behind me with a heavy groan. I'm lead up the stairwell and into a hall. Squinting against the bright lights, I watch Ronan disappear down a corridor. Finally, after twists and turns, I'm shoved into a room after him.

The men leave, closing the doors, and silence descends like an ominous mist. The furnishings in the room are sparse: a few leather couches and a pool table at the far end. I stand by the door as Ronan walks over to the open fire that's roaring away. He watches it for a moment, tension building like a pending volcanic eruption. He clasps his hands behind his back and crosses the room, taking a seat on one of the leather chairs. There's a chess board laid out on the small table beside him, and he plucks a piece off the board and studies it. His silence causes my stomach to twist nervously.

"Why do you not value your life?" he asks without looking at me. I can hear the strain in his voice.

"I wouldn't say that I don't value it." I move over to the fire and stare at the flames as they lick over the logs. "Simply that some things are more important." I glance over my shoulder at him.

"So," he places the chess piece back on the board and smooths his hand down the front of his shirt, "what you are saying, is you wish for me to kill you then?" He smiles.

I shrug one shoulder and take a breath. His face appears calm, but it's in that eerie calmness that his anger is palpable. I can only hazard a guess that Gabe did what I asked. After all, Ronan doesn't get angry. It's beneath him. It would take something momentous to rile him like this. "No. But make no mistake, I would rather die than roll over and play the helpless bitch."

"Oh," a sick laugh rumbles from his chest, "you haven't played the helpless bitch since you've been here. But, I will say," he pushes to his feet, "you have played the role of the *stupid* bitch very well." He stalks toward me, trailing his fingers along the wall beside the fireplace with his eyes locked on mine. "Haven't you?" he says, and my heart goes into a sprint.

"That's a matter of opinion," I say, watching him carefully.

He laughs again as he reaches for something, and before I can even register what he's doing, I feel warm metal across my throat. He pins me to the wall, the reflection of the fire dancing in his eyes. His jaw twitches and the pressure over my throat increases as he leans in toward me. I struggle for breath, grabbing at the metal fire poker he has rammed against my throat, gagging and choking as he pushes me up the wall until my feet are lifted from the floor.

"Is it a matter of opinion, Camilla? Because I would think having your brother take a shipment of mine would be nothing *but* stupidity. You've had enough time around me to know better, surely?"

My vision blurs and my eyes water. I claw at him; at anything I can reach. My pulse pounds like an unwanted warning alarm in my ears.

A sadistic grin spreads over his lips before he leans next to my ear. "I thought you weren't afraid of death, little kitty," he laughs before snatching the rod away, dropping me to a heap on the floor.

I cough and rub at my bruised throat. "There are better ways to go." I cough again, sucking in several deep breaths. "I can't be held responsible for what Gabriel does."

"You killed my men, ruined one of my cars." He stares down at me. "And then you obviously contact your brother. This had very little to do with Gabriel." He bends over, grabbing the hair by my scalp and lifting me to my feet. "But it does now..." He drags me to a chair and shoves me down just as the door opens. Igor steps in with an open laptop and places it on the pool table, spinning it around to face me.

There, on the screen, is Gabriel. Both his eyes have swollen shut, and his face is covered in blood. A man punches him with a knuckle duster. Gabe's head snaps to the side, and he spits blood before laughing. "Hey, sis," he smirks.

"You look like shit," I say.

"Eh, fucking Russian putas." A guy punches him in the gut. Gabe bends down where I can't see him, choking. I'm pretty sure he's throwing up. They keep beating him, and I force myself not to react even though the sight of my brother hurt pulls at something deep inside me. I clench my jaw. *This is the life we chose. I have to suck it up.*

Ronan stands behind me, his finger slowly tracing over my bruised neck. He leans down by my ear. "I do so love the way bruises look on your tanned skin," he whispers. "So pretty, little kitty." Goosebumps prickle over my body as his warm breath skates over my throat.

A guy shoves Gabriel back into his chair, and grabs a handful of his hair, forcing him to look right at the camera. Right at me. Ronan wraps my hair around his wrist and yanks my head to the side. His lips sweep along the side of my neck, and Gabriel growls on the video. I force myself to remain still. I'm not sure whether it's because I want to pull away from Ronan, or lean into him. I don't trust myself with him...especially not in front of my brother. Ronan's hand creeps over my shoulder, across my collarbone, right to the top of my breast, and then he nibbles at my ear.

"Your pink pussy looked so pretty wrapped around the barrel of my gun the other day." He exhales. "Makes me think I want to fuck you myself."

I stare back at Gabe for a second, hoping he'll understand what I'm about to do before I turn to face Ronan. Our lips brush, and I drop my gaze to his lips. "You won't fuck me, Russian. It threatens your precious control too much," I say before I swipe my tongue over my bottom lip.

Laughing, he traces his tongue down my throat. "I could have one of my men fuck you while I watch. While you scream, begging for me to make them stop."

"Oh, please, Ronan." I roll my eyes. "No." I place my hand to my chest, and he moves out from behind me.

"Gabriel," he says just before the man on the screen punches my brother again. "You were being such an obedient servant. I'm going to handle your sister while my men take care of you. Next time, I will slit her throat and let the other cartels handle the man who sold out to, how do you say it?" He taps his finger over his chin, "The fucking Russian?"

Igor closes the screen, scoops the laptop off the table, and leaves, closing the door behind him. Ronan turns back to me, smiling as he unfastens his cufflinks and meticulously rolls the white sleeves of his dress shirt to his elbows. "Now, how do I punish the fearless?" he asks, taking a seat behind the chess board. He picks up a pawn, twisting it in his hand before places it on the board. "Rape will do nothing, so that's out of the question..." He moves another chess piece. "Torture?" He shrugs. "Overrated, don't you think?"

I cross the room and take a seat opposite him. "I find it effective on the weak."

He cocks a brow before he unfastens the buttons of his shirt. "You're not weak."

"No." I look up at him through my lashes and smile.

"Get undressed," he says.

I stare at him a beat longer. One minute he wants to kill me and now he wants me naked. If it's humiliation he wants then he'll be bitterly disappointed. I stand up and grab the hem of the oversized shirt Igor threw at me when he dumped me in that basement. I'm naked underneath so this is a short strip tease. It drops at my feet and I lift a brow at him before I sit down and cross my legs. "You know, there are much more exciting ways to get a girl naked."

A smug smile inches over his lips as his eyes drag over my naked body. "Do you enjoy sex, Camilla?"

"No." I flash him an incredulous look. "I'm a fucking virgin."

"Do you prefer it when a man chokes you from behind as he takes you, when he treats you like a dirty slut?" He grins. "I'd imagine you do."

"I won't *let* a man do anything, but if he can take it..." I narrow my eyes and trail my finger slowly up my naked thigh. "Could *you* take it, Ronan? I'd imagine you could."

"I take everything I want, Camilla. You should know better." He pushes to his feet and slowly circles behind me, sweeping my hair from my neck. "You should."

"Maybe I just like to have the point driven home." I shouldn't like this; I should hate everything about him. He just had my brother beaten in front of me, but I love the violence of it all. I love the way he exercises his iron-will without mercy. I love the throbbing in my throat, and I can imagine the pretty bruise already forming there. I like that he's marked me in a singular moment where he lost a grip on that precious control. I love having that power over him, the same way he has this power over me.

He grabs my hair, fisting it as he jerks my head back so hard my teeth knock against each other. "Is that why you are so defiant? Hmm?" He leans down, skirting his nose along my neck, inhaling and groaning. "Because you like it rough?"

"Maybe I just like to defy you, to see what you'll do." I turn my face toward him. My scalp screams in protest at the unyielding grip he has on my hair. "Watching you lose control...it would be so beautiful." His breath washes over my face, and I fight back a moan as the intoxicating scent of his cigar-laced clothes wraps around me. I wish he didn't affect me like this, but he does, and I refuse to be a victim to it. He lets go of my hair, and I stand up, rounding the chair and forcing my body against his. "So utterly destructive."

His lips press against the corner of my mouth. "If I lose control, everything around me burns, Krasivaya."

My pulse hammers through my veins. "I *do* love fire," I whisper. His hands skim along my sides in a feather light touch before he leans in and bites my lip hard enough to draw blood. His tongue sweeps over the damaged flesh and a soft groan rumbles from his chest.

"And I do love the *taste* of blood." His fingers dig into my hips, and he backs me across the room. I find myself fantasizing about what it would be like to have him fuck me, to have him completely dominate me, ruin me. A man like Ronan Cole, with so much power, such depravity running through his veins—it would surely be an experience of a lifetime. My legs bump against the smooth wood of the pool table and he grabs my waist, lifting me and setting me on the edge. I swallow in an effort to steady my racing pulse.

"I just had your brother tortured." He steps between my legs, crowding me. "I just choked you against a wall and had you strip for me. You know I'm a monster and yet, I know you're soaking wet for me right now, Camilla."

I glide my hand up the front of his chest and around the back of his neck. "What does that make me?" I ask, succumbing to my addiction and nipping his jaw.

"Sick." He rubs his lip over my cheek, his hold on my hips tightening. "So very sick, little kitty."

My fingers dig into his neck until I'm sure my nails bite into his skin. The expensive material of his shirt brushes against my bare breast, and my nipples tighten painfully. Our lips are so close; I could tilt my chin and I'd be kissing him. I press my free hand against his lower stomach and slide my way down until I'm cupping a very big, very hard cock. I scratch my nails over the material of his pants and a low rumble works up his throat as his dick twitches.

"This is the only true power there is, Ronan," I say on a smile.

A knowing grin shapes his lips as his fingers dance over my breasts, my stomach, my thigh. I fight to keep my legs from falling shamelessly open and inviting him in, because I want him to touch me. And I hate him all the more for it. I keep my eyes locked on his, watching the lust swirl within them. One of his warm fingers swipes over my clit and I bite down on my lip, stifling the moan. His stance widens between my thighs, his gaze falling to my pussy before it slowly moves back to my face.

"Is it?" He whispers, shoving his fingers so deep and hard inside me that my entire body is thrust back onto the pool table. My hands knock the balls across the felt when I catch myself. His fingers bend and flex inside me, coaxing a moan before he pulls his hand free. "*That* is power," he says on a smirk and slips his fingers between his full lips. "Mm." He arches a brow. “Now, get dressed for dinner.” And with that, he turns and leaves the room.

I fall back against the felt tabletop, my lungs straining to catch a full breath. Fuck Ronan Cole. I don't know how much longer I can do this with him.

Chapter 22

Ronan

"Animal" – Bad Flower

The smell of her pussy is still on my fingers when I push her door open. Camilla's standing in front of the mirror, dressed in a red satin dress. She gives me a fleeting look over her shoulder, before turning back to the mirror and tracing her lips with red lipstick. *Anastasia should be delighted with this.*

"Aren't you the vision of beauty," I say.

She turns to face me again, propping her hip against the dresser. "Where are we going?" The condescending tone to her voice does make me happy because I got to her, and it utterly delights me.

"To a nice dinner with the President and new Prime Minister."

"Oh, I do so love Anastasia's thrilling company."

"She's sure to love yours." I snap my fingers. Two men come in from the hallway and Camilla glares at me like an angry cat before they grab her.

"What the fuck is this?" she asks, backing away as they approach.

I glance at my watch as they cart her to the bed, kicking and screaming. "A little gift from me to you, and gentlemen," I say, tapping the face of my watch, "time is of the essence. Do try to not mess up her hair, it looks so lovely."

They pin her down and, of course, she fights them like a wild animal, spitting insults in Spanish.

"Camilla?" I sing. "I said not to mess up your hair." I step toward the end of the bed, smiling at her. She does look so beautiful pinned down like that.

"I will kill you, Russian!" One of the men grabs her chin and she turns her head, sinking her teeth into his forearm.

"I'm certain if you could, you would, but..." I toss my hands up on a laugh before I lean down next to her and pet over her head. "Shh, little kitty. It will be okay." I look up at Donovan and nod. He takes a scalpel and cuts a small slice in the side of her neck. She snarls at the pain, and my grin widens. He uses tweezers to shove the small chip underneath the flap of meat before he quickly stiches her up.

"Now," I say, holding up a finger, "before they let you go, I must warn you, you may want to really think through any more rebellious acts you have planned."

"What the fuck did you just do?" Her face is red with anger, her nostrils flaring.

"Made you mine." I beam. "The small chip that was just sewn into your neck... you defy me again, I'll press a button that will cause the outer layer to disintegrate, expelling a toxic compound into your blood stream. It will melt you from the inside out, shutting down your organs one by one." I sigh. "Festive, wouldn't you agree?" I snap my fingers again and the two men release her.

She bolts upright, then charges toward me as she swings her arm back. I catch her arm mid-strike. "Camilla," I say, squeezing her delicate wrist, "You must know I'm not a man who makes empty threats. Do learn to control yourself."

She steps closer, pressing her breasts against me. Her eyes flick to my mouth and a smug grin dances across her lips. "I promise you, one day I will kill you, Russian, and I will piss on your cold, dead body." She brings her lips to my ear. "I'm not a *woman* who makes empty threats."

"Yes, yes." I circle my finger in the air and she glares at me. "Turn around." Her eyes flame before she spins on her heel. I grab the thick, diamond choker from my pocket and delicately place it around her neck, covering the tiny stitches. "Can't have you looking like Frankenstein," I say.

"Well, I wouldn't if you didn't put shit in my neck," she says with a growl. I grab her arm to lead her from the room, and she snatches away from me. "So what? I misbehave and you'll kill me?" A masochistic smile spreads across her face.

I don't respond, simply lead her out of the room, down

the hallway and through the front door to the waiting car.

The ballroom is filled with politicians and bankers welcoming Anton as the new Prime Minister, and here Camilla stands at my side, a silent rage radiating from her. I loop her arm through mine as we cross the room. "That necklace looks lovely on you," I whisper.

"Fuck off, Russian," she says under her breath.

I pat my hand over hers and smile as we step up to Anton. He's rigid when I shake his hand, nervous. "Congratulations on your new office, Prime Minister."

"Thank you," he says, but I hear the regret in his tone. The toll his greed has taken on him shows in the purple circles below his eyes, the gloss of sweat on his brow. Some men think they can handle guilt. Most can't. Anton thought he could shrug off his responsibility in Vasily's assassination, but I guess he underestimated the weight of guilt. Such a shame. His eyes shift to Camilla before another politician, Demetri Sokolov—my choice for the next President of Russia—steps beside us to shake Anton's hand.

Demetri glances at me from the corner of his eye, and I feel Anton shrink away from us both. The designer suit Demetri has on gives him a refined edge, but no amount of money or Versace can dull the psychotic flicker within his eyes.

"Ah, Demetri." I turn to shake his hand. "So good to see you."

"And you, Ronan," he says, his attention turning to Camilla. Lust swims in his eyes as his gaze drags over her curves, and my jaw tightens. "May I have a word, Ronan?"

“Of course.” I slip my arm around Camilla's waist as I escort her across the lavish ballroom and down a corridor beside the stairs, Demetri following. We stop by a large oil painting and I turn to face him. His eyes lock on Camilla as he lights a cigarette. "Camilla," I say, "this is Demetri Solkolov, the soon to be President of Russia." I watch her eyes narrow. I can almost see her mind rolling through the possibilities.

"The pleasure is all mine." Demetri takes her hand and slightly bows his head before glancing over at me. "This is taking longer than you promised."

"Assassinations can be unpredictable, Demetri," I say. "You should know that by now, and besides, there's one final detail that needs to be tended to." I arch a brow.

Smoke billows through his lips. "The money should show up tomorrow."

"Excellent, don't forget to repay yourself from the lovely taxpayers of Russia once you're in office." I chuckle. "Your missile shall be delivered within the week, and I have so enjoyed doing business with you."

My chest swells with pride, excitement, but I won't get ahead of myself. I know all too well that pulling off a scandal of this proportion cannot be celebrated until all is said and done. And even then, having vile, power-hungry men I own sitting on seats of authority is merely just the beginning.

He walks away and I catch sight of Anastasia standing across the ballroom. The pout on her face screams of hurt even though she's clutching to her husband's arm like a doting wife. I pretend not to notice her and turn my attention to Camilla, trailing my fingers over her neck. The slightest hint of a bruise peeks from the sparkling choker, and I can't help but remember how unhinged it felt when I pinned her against the wall with that fire poker. I brush my finger over the bruise before my gaze shifts to her red lips. So full and perfect. All I can think about is taking her bottom lip between my teeth and drawing blood again. The thought sends a surge of adrenaline through me and I take a step toward her, pinning her between my body and the wall.

"Ronan." A fire dances in her eyes, and I don't know if it's a warning or an invitation. I'd take either...

I brush my lips over her warm cheek and grab her hips, squeezing as I force her harder against the wall. "Pretend you don't want this," I whisper as I skim my mouth over her throat, groaning next to her ear.

She cups my jaw, and rakes her nails down the side of my neck. "What do you want me to say, Russian?" she breathes.

"Not a single thing." I fist her hair and slam my mouth over hers, parting her lips with my tongue. And my, her lips do feel so inviting. Her body goes rigid against mine, then she shoves at my chest.

"Seriously? You just put a thing in my neck like a pet bitch –"

"Oh, Camilla..." I tighten my hold in her hair until she flinches. "When will you realize, I own you?" I press my lips back over hers, knowing that Anastasia is watching and breaking into a million pieces at this very moment.

Camilla snarls before sinking her teeth into my bottom lip. Blood wells in my mouth, and I smile against her lips. And that's when I feel that slight give, the moment where her body goes just a little limp in my hold. She bites at my lip again, sending a sharp twinge of pain shooting through me followed by the instinct to hurt her. My hand goes from her hair to her throat, my fingers wrapping tightly around her before I break away from the kiss and rest my forehead against hers, my hand still clutching her throat. I want to kiss her, hurt her, fuck her. Cut her...

I stare at her blush stained cheeks, my chest heaving while her pulse thrums beneath my fingertips. Her eyes flicker with hate and lust. The sight of my blood smeared across her lips makes my cock swell. "Before this is all over," I say in her ear, "you'll beg for me."

"Never," she whispers on a smile. "You already have too much power, Russian."

She drags a finger along my bottom lip. When she moves her hand away, I spot a smudge of blood on her finger. Her eyes lock with mine as she slips her bloodied finger between her lips. If I had an ounce less control, we'd both be in trouble. Not much in this life can make me weak, but this... Within her eyes lie cruel promises of violence and lust. And that strikes something buried so reverently deep inside me— there is every possibility this woman may be my undoing. It shouldn't be such a thrill.

Inhaling, I loop her arm through mine and lead her through the room. We make our way to the dinner table, and I tell myself I must deny these blood-filled urges.

Chapter 23

Camilla

"The Devil You Know" – X Ambassadors

Ronan pulls my chair out and I sit before he takes the seat beside me. My heart is still racing and my lips are still tingling, but Ronan just strikes up a conversation with the man next to him as if absolutely nothing happened. I pick up the glass of wine in front of me and down it in one gulp. The steak knife on the table catches my attention, and I picture myself picking it up and ramming it into Ronan's jugular. That should give him enough blood...

As if he can read my mind, he glances at me, lifting a brow at my empty wine glass. A waiter passes by and I hold the glass up, staring at Ronan as the man fills it again. When I raise it to my lips, Ronan takes it from me. Chardonnay splashes over his hand.

"Behave," he says as he strokes my hair behind my ear. There's a sudden, sharp pain that shoots through my neck when his thumb brushes the small incision on my throat. Something uncomfortable settles in my stomach. I've been kidnapped, beaten, tortured, raped, and for some reason that implant feels more inhuman and barbaric than all of it. He's reduced me to an animal simpering beneath his will. I know he's bad, but I thought he was better than this. He brought a gun to a knife fight. And for some reason, as strange as it is, I find myself disappointed with him. I twist out of his hold and he smiles before dropping his hand.

The man next to me attempts to lure me into conversation, but I simply ignore him and drink half my glass of wine. The entire party fades to background noise as my mind drifts, dredging up memories I try my best to ignore. I jump when Ronan touches my hand, pulling it away from my neck. I hadn't even realized I was touching it. The men at the table discuss something, but of course I can’t understand a word they say. Annoyed, I glance around the room and spot Anastasia a few tables over glaring at us. I hate Ronan, but I hate that cunt more. I paint a smile on my lips before I turn to Ronan and trace my fingers over the back of his neck. His brows pinch in a frown. Even the thought of Anastasia's rage isn't enough to override the plummeting feeling tearing through me, that fissure of disappointed hurt that I want to cut out like a disease.

"I need to use the bathroom," I whisper and push my chair back.

I move to stand and Ronan grips my jaw, forcing me to hover just above my chair. He stares at me for a second before grazing his lips over mine in a whisper of a touch.

“Don’t be long.”

My nostrils flare as I pull away from his hold and straighten up. I hurry to the restroom, shove the door open, and go straight to the mirror. Taking a deep breath, I brace my hands on the vanity before I glance up at the mirror and pull the diamond choker down inspecting the small incision on the side of my neck. The black thread looks like spider legs crawling out of my skin. The door pushes open and the noise from the ballroom spills inside. I keep looking in the mirror, paying no attention to the woman stopped at the sink. That is, until I feel her gaze on me. I turn. *Anastasia. Great.*

"You know he's in love with me?" she says, her eyes watering.

I throw my head back on a groan and pray for patience with this bullshit. "The same way you're in love with your husband?"

She inhales, her cheeks turning red. "You’re too plain for a man like him. You do understand that?"

"Okay, Skeletor." I laugh and take a step toward her. She, of course, takes a small step back. "If I'm so plain then why are you in the bathroom throwing your skinny ass around?" I eye her up and down before turning back to my reflection and running my fingers through my hair. She's still glaring at me in the mirror. "A lion doesn't need to roar to let you know it's a lion,” I say. “You're a politician's house cat, Anastasia."

"And from the looks of it, you're nothing but an expensive whore."

"From the woman doing the dirty on her husband?" Grinning, I cock a brow at her.

"If you know what's best for you, you'll leave him alone."

I snort. *This bitch.* "Oh, I don't think he wants to be left alone." I face her and prop my hip against the vanity. "In fact, he very much wants my company. In every single way." I bite my bottom lip on a smile.

Her eyes flash and my grin deepens just before a loud smack echoes around the restroom. My cheek stings, and Anastasia spins on her heel to leave. Closing my eyes, I inhale a calming breath but it doesn't work. My temper snaps like a band pulled too tight. In a heartbeat, I have my hand in her bleached hair. She squeals, and I pull back so hard that her back bows before she's forced to her knees.

"Understand this," I whisper as I round her. "I may look like Ronan Cole's latest arm candy, but push me again and I will snap your skinny-fucking-neck like the pathetic slut you are." A small whimper slips through her lips before I yank her head back further. "Are we crystal clear?" Tears pour down her face, smudging her mascara. I hiss a breath through my teeth.

"Yes," she breathes.

"Good." I throw her messy hair out of my hand and she scrambles to her feet, rushing from the bathroom.

My pulse races. My chest heaves. I lean against the vanity to calm the red-hot anger beating away at me like a caged beast. Anastasia was the last straw. I'm out of control, completely at a loss for the first time in my life because Ronan Cole has so utterly removed it from me. I can't fight back without him pulling the plug with this stupid thing in my neck. I'm not afraid of death, but it has to be on my terms, not his. Whirling around, I stare at my reflection before I unfasten the choker at my throat and wrap it around my hand. I swing my arm back and ram my fist into the mirror. The glass shatters beneath the diamonds, splintering my reflection. Pieces of mirror fall into the sink. Some scatter across the tile. I grab a shard from the sink and toss the necklace to the floor.

Someone must have heard that. I imagine a worker will be coming in here at any moment so I slip into one of the stalls and lock the door. This is going to be a bitch, so I sit on the toilet and take a breath as I feel over the small stitches in my throat. My hand trembles as I place the glass to my neck and work the sharp point over the delicate threads. Jolts of pain radiate through me each time I accidently slice my skin. Blood slicks my fingers as I fumble through severing the stitches. They finally pop loose and warm liquid trickles down my neck.

The bathroom door creaks open. There's the steady click of shoes as someone crosses the tile.

"Little kitty..." Ronan coos, "Come out, come out,

wherever you are." The door to the first stall bangs against the wall and I cringe.

I press my fingers against the wound in my neck and take another deep breath. Forcing my nails into the cut, I ignore the churn in my stomach and the dizzy feeling in my mind. More blood gushes down my neck, gliding over my collar bone and catching on my dress.

The doors bang open one by one before there's a thud on the other side of the door I'm facing. "Jesus, I can't pee now?" I snap. I shove my fingers deeper into the gash until my nails scrape something tiny and hard. The pain is blinding. A sharp breath claws up my throat. *Just a couple more centimeters.*

He taps over the door. "Come out, Camilla."

I catch a hold of whatever the fuck he put inside me and try to pry it free from my neck, hissing at the pain. When I finally tug the metal chip out of my neck, I tear half my flesh away with it. I let out a heavy breath and collapse against the tank panting. The steady trickle of blood runs down my neck, and there's something oddly comforting about its warmth.

"Open the door."

I stand up and lift the lid, dropping the bloodied microchip into the water before I flush the toilet. I unlock the door and yank it open, coming face to face with Ronan. His gaze slowly drops to my neck, his cheeks reddening, and I can't help but smirk.

"You would..." He takes a step inside the stall, backing me against the cold wall. "I almost think you crave punishment." Grabbing both my wrists, he pins them to the wall above my head.

"As long as it's the old-fashioned way," I breathe. Anger and sheer dominance pour off him. My body hums in anticipation as he presses his body against mine.

One corner of his mouth tugs up. "Mm," he hums leaning in by my neck. The heat of his breath caresses the side of my throat, and I find myself closing my eyes at the feeling. "You want me to hurt you *almost* as much as I want to hurt you," he whispers before I feel his tongue drag along the side of my neck—right over the open wound. His hold on my wrists tightens, his fingers twitching as he places his lips over the cut and groans.

I bow against him, my head tilting to the side as a shameless moan slips past my lips. He's sick and awful, so what does that make me? I should be repulsed by him, but with each terrible thing he does, I only crave him more. He's a disturbing addiction that I wish I could quit, but know I would miss every single day.

His nose skims along my jawline as he drags his lips over my cheek. "Your blood almost tastes as good as your pussy."

My head spins, my legs tremble. I close my eyes and touch my forehead to his. "Show me," I whisper. I crave this toxic depravity. He's my downfall and I want him. I want it.

His eyes dance with promises of pain and blood and everything I want so much, and then his lips slam over mine. Hard, brutal. His tongue brushes mine, and I savor the metallic taste of the blood staining his lips. I moan and then, he's gone.

I open my eyes and Ronan's at the sink, wiping the blood from his face with the back of his hand. And here I am, pressed against the wall because I'm afraid if I try to stand on my own I'll fall. Without as much as a glance in my direction, he steps into the hall. I go to the sink, grab a hand towel, and press it against my neck. He's like a tornado and I know I should move out of his path, but every time he approaches I find myself standing still, wanting to get swept up in those dangerous winds.

The door to the restroom flies open again. Ronan's speaking to someone in Russian, anger lacing his voice before he steps back inside, holding my coat out. I slip my arms through the sleeves and he adjusts the collar, his eyes trained on the wound. "You do know that I'll just have another chip placed in your neck. If you rip that out. Another. And another. I will kill you, Camilla, but I won't do it just yet. How humane your death is, well," he narrows his eyes, "that's up to you."

I close my eyes, unable to look at him. "Please don't," I whisper. My eyes flash open. "Put a bullet in my head, fuck me, beat me, whatever you want. But please don't do that again." I awkwardly rub my hand over my forearm, and his eyes flicker with a sadistic pleasure. I hate that I'm reduced to begging— that this one, simple act bothers me so much and now he knows it. "We both know I'll die here in your shitty country, but at least let me go down fighting." I look him over. "Or perhaps you like easy prey, Russian. I didn't take you for the type."

His finger swipes along my cheek, his eyes trained on my lips. "You are not easy prey, Krasivaya." Without another word, he threads his fingers through mine and leads me into the hall.

People stare as we pass. Even with the coat I guess they can see the blood. A man stops Ronan, speaking in muffled Russian as he flashes concerned glances my way. Ronan responds, and all I can make out is Anastasia's name. The man gasps and places a hand on his chest, and Ronan ushers me from the hotel and into the limo waiting outside.

The door closes and I glare at him. "If you just told him that bitch hurt me, I swear to god..." I press my fingers to my neck and they come away crimson. *Jesus, how deep did he put that thing?*

His fingers drum over his knee as he stares through the window.

"Why *are* you fucking her?" I ask, and he sighs in exasperation.

"Why did you fuck Jésus?" He turns to look at me. "You *should* understand..."

"Jésus was my enemy. I keep my enemies close." I

glare at him. "I can't imagine Anastasia is your enemy, Ronan." I skim my gaze over his chest. "Maybe you just like the wifey types. You can tell me."

"*Camilla*," he leans across to me, "you truly know nothing about me, so how would you know who I consider an enemy?"

"Cryptic," I muse. "You're not very likeable. Surely everyone is your enemy, but I don't see you sinking your dick in half of Russia."

"You've yet to see me sink my dick into anything." He smiles before he turns his attention back out the window.

"With your taste in women...I'm good."

"Jealousy is not an attractive quality on you."

I laugh. "Russian, jealousy is an emotion experienced only over something one wants or is possessive of."

"Yes—I know." I can almost hear the smirk in his voice.

"You know," I roll my eyes. "You should go and see someone about that god complex of yours."

In true Ronan fashion, he simply ignores me. I know he's angry. Hell, I'm surprised the people out on the street can't feel it, but he hides it behind semi-civil conversation. Heaven forbid anyone should know that his precious control is slipping. But I can almost see it, his fingertips clinging to that delicate edge. Again, the thought of how beautifully devastating it would be to watch him fray and splinter pops into my mind. He would be like a category five hurricane colliding with civilization, destroying everything in his wake without mercy.

Ronan can keep his secrets, but if that blonde bitch comes at me again I will snap her neck. President's wife or not.

Chapter 24

Ronan

"Control" - Halsey

Oh, the dilemma I am in...

Defiant doesn't touch what Camilla is, and, if I am honest with myself, I almost respect her will to rebel. *Almost.* I spend the entire ride home contemplating what to do with her, but what do you do with someone whose arrogance and pride override any rational drive to survive? Then again, Camilla is not stupid, she knows how this business works. She knows that once I'm done with her death awaits.

As soon as we're inside my house, Igor takes her coat. I grab her by the elbow, escort her to my office, and lock the door behind me before I make my way toward the roaring fireplace. "You know there are consequences to what you've done?" *But what consequences, I'm still not certain.*

She sighs. "I'd expect nothing less."

If I put another chip in her she'll just dig it out. Then I'd be forced to kill her, and I'm not ready yet. I circle around her, trailing my fingers over her shoulders as I debate on the proper form of humiliation. Camilla is not the type of woman who will find degradation in being beaten or fucked. The things that would make most women cringe, she wouldn't bat an eye at, but... The ring on my right hand glints in the firelight and a sick smile works over my lips. "The next chip will be placed much deeper," I say, wanting nothing more but to wind her up.

"Then I'll cut that one out, too," she says through gritted teeth.

"What if I place it here?" I sweep my hand over the middle of her back. "How would you cut that out?"

"I'm extremely flexible, and I don't mind scars."

My eyes drop to the healing wounds on her chest and my cock swells. "You'd rather I beat you, wouldn't you?"

"Yes."

I lean down by her neck. "Fuck you?" I ask, and she tilts her head to the side, inviting me closer. "What is it about that chip that bothers you so much?"

She whirls around and locks eyes with me. For a moment, there's a glint of vulnerability. "I want to die on my terms."

"There are only my terms here," I breathe against her neck.

Her lips graze over my jaw before her teeth scrape my ear. "A soldier's death then. You can give me that much, Ronan."

The way my name rolls from her tongue causes a slight groan to rumble up my throat. "The way you behave has everything to do with how you die." I grab the tongs from the fireplace and slip my ring from my finger, looking at the raised letters on its surface. My initials will look so lovely burned onto her skin, and she'll hate that I've branded her like livestock. "Take off your dress. Bend over the desk."

Her eyes dance with defiance for a moment before she slowly unzips her dress. The material slides down her body until she's standing in nothing but a black lace bra and thong. The glow of the flames dance over her curves. She turns and bends over the desk, spreading her legs as she brushes her hair over her shoulder.

I move the fire screen and grip the ring with the tongs, holding it in the fire until the metal burns bright red. I step up behind her and place my palm over the side of her face, pinning her to the desk.

"What are you doing?" She thrashes against my hold. "Ronan, what are you doing?" Her voice rises with panic as I place the hot metal below her ear. The skin sizzles and pops, but she doesn't scream, she barely even winces as a small plume of smoke rises from her neck. She is strong, I'll give her that. I hold the ring to her skin, my eyes trailing over the morbid tattoo on her back.

I drop the tongs to the floor, staring at my initials blackened over her skin as I sweep my hand over her back. Instead of smooth skin, my fingers play over ridges. *Scars from burns*. So many layers to peel back. “How very pretty,” I whisper, fisting her hair as I lean over her. "It doesn't matter what I do because you’re not afraid of death, and without fear, you won't submit, which is admirable. It truly is, but you are defiant." I yank her head back. "So defiant, Camilla, and the thing that you have yet to understand is that you can do and say what you want, but at the end of the day you *are* mine. You want to die on your own terms, but that is impossible. How do you not see that?"

"Oh, it riles you, doesn't it?" she snarls, fighting against me. "That you can't control every facet of me, that you can't force my hand."

"That is where you are very wrong, Camilla." I laugh. "If you take your own life, it's due to me. It’s solely because of the control I have over you."

"Don't flatter yourself."

Her absolute disregard for death incites me. Her blatant disrespect enrages me. Her volatile personality entices me. I shouldn't enjoy this, but I do in every carnal way possible. "The fact that you are so powerless destroys you, doesn't it?"

"Maybe I secretly like it." She presses her ass against me, and the corner of her lips pull into a smug grin.

"I know you do," I whisper, sweeping my finger over the freshly burned flesh on her neck. She hisses out a breath. "Ownership does look so pretty on you."

"Men are so predictable. All of you wanting to own

pretty things."

I simply smirk at her before placing a soft kiss to the corner of her mouth. "Such a pretty little pet," I say, wanting to provoke her anger, her rage. I want her mad because it makes my cock throb.

"I swear Russian," she snarls and thrashes against me, "before this is all said and done, I will make you bleed."

"Such *sweet* promises," I whisper, trailing my palm over the curve of her ass. Her warm skin serves as such a temptation, but her anger even more. No matter how powerful a man may be, things as primitive as this—the scent of a woman's skin, the promise of her tight pussy—it's a weakness rarely avoided. Closing my eyes, I imagine her pinned underneath me, my hands on her throat as I bury myself inside her. But I can't give her that satisfaction. If anything, I want to rip the one thing she feels she has power over away, so I let my fingers slip underneath the lace of her thong. My finger skims her asshole and she moans. "When I take this, I will make you bleed," I groan, circling my finger over her hole before I slide it down to her wet pussy. "So aroused, little kitty," I murmur against her cheek, playing with her. Each swipe of my finger makes my cock ache for her, but this is about control. Power. Ownership.

I bury two fingers inside her so hard, so fast, she gasps. "I think you like to be treated like a dirty slut, Camilla. You crave the depraved." I nip at her ear before I place my thumb on her asshole and push it inside. She clenches around me, groaning and shoving back against me. Using my free hand, I smash her face against the desk as I finger fuck her, more than delighted at the way she claws at the hard wood between deep pants.

"Shit," she whispers. She tightens around my fingers. Her movements grow desperate. But I can't allow her to come. I pull out of her and step away. She's bent over and spread out on my desk on the verge of an orgasm she'll never have, and I find so much pleasure in that.

An exasperated breath rushes from her lips before she turns over and sits up. She scoots to the edge of the desk. I admire the lovely flush painted on her cheeks. She closes her eyes for a second and when she opens them there's a wild flicker. "You know what they say..." Her legs spread open and her hand drops between her thighs, underneath the lace. "If you want a job done properly..."

Smiling, I cross the room and snatch her hand away. "That's not allowed."

"Oh, Ronan." She inches toward me, sweeping her lips over mine. "So uptight all the time." Her lips trail over my cheek, and then she pinches the skin of my jaw between her teeth. "Don't pretend you don't want to watch my pussy clench around my fingers, or better yet, feel it on your cock."

"Why would I want that, Camilla?" I pull her hand toward my lips and slip her wet fingers into my mouth, sucking the delicate taste of her pussy from them. I want nothing more at this moment than to fuck her... "Are you going to be bad?"

"I'll take those as rhetorical questions."

I walk around the desk and open a drawer, pulling a thin rope out. "Turn around," I say.

"You just happen to keep rope in your desk? Like a damn serial killer," she mumbles, hopping off the desk and turning around on a sigh.

I take both her wrists and loop the rope around them. I fully expect her to be out of these within the hour, but it's just the principle of it really. The degradation, the forced submission from such an angry jungle cat. "Now then. Let's go." I grab hold of the rope, escorting her from my office to her room.

When we reach her doorway she turns to glare at me, and I offer her a charming smile. "I do hope you have delightful dreams." And with that, I close the door.

Camilla has added a certain level of...*entertainment* to my life. She makes me angry, she reduces me to the most primitive of wants, but in the end, I control her and that is immeasurably satisfying. It is so tragic to think I'll have to kill her once it's all over, but at the same time, I know she will be utterly beautiful when she bleeds.

Chapter 25

Camilla

"Hook, Line & Sinker" – Royal Blood

The door clicks shut and I bite back a frustrated groan. My shoulders ache, my neck stings, and my pussy throbs. *God, he's an asshole.* I glance around the room, looking for anything I can use to get out of this damn rope. I shove the lamp off the bedside table, watching as the ceramic base shatters. Glass dusts the floor and I crouch down, pushing my hands into the top of the broken lamp base. My teeth snap together when the sharp edges shred the side of my hand. As if I haven't bled enough today. I awkwardly rub the rope against the jagged porcelain, feeling it catch and loosen bit by bit. I smile when the rope finally pops free. My hands are covered in blood, and I have to pluck tiny bits of ceramic out of my hands and wrists. Ronan can go fuck himself—and he can watch me fuck myself. *Not allowed, please!* I walk to the corner of the room, hop up on the dresser, and adjust the camera until I'm pretty sure it's focused on the bed.

I strut back across to the bed and slowly slide my lace thong over my hips and down my legs. Blood from my hands and wrists streak my skin, but I don't care. If anything, I like it. And I'm sure that sick bastard will like it, too. Lying on the bed, I spread my legs wide and angle myself toward that camera with its blinking red light. Ronan will probably never see this, but I'll pretend he will. The thought of Ronan sitting in some dark room watching me stroke myself while I'm covered in blood...well, it shouldn't turn me on as much as it does.

I trail my bloodied hand along the inside of my thigh. As soon as my finger brushes over my pussy I throw my head back and close my eyes. I push my fingers inside, and imagine they're Ronan's. I remember the way he brutally slammed his hand into me, pushing his thumb into my ass like a conquistador wishing to soil every part of me. And oh, how I want him to.

He's right. I like the depravity of it, the wrongness. I fuck myself, pulling my fingers out and swirling over my clit until my back arches off the bed. My mind conjures filthy, erotic images of Ronan owning me, taking what he wants. A moan slips from my lips as a shudder tears from my body. I imagine Ronan fucking me, cutting me and a wave of heat drowns me. I come with his name on my lips, letting it all loose, because I want him to hear. I want him to know what he missed, what his precious control is costing him. I lie here gasping and panting and hating myself a little bit, because I've always been drawn to the things I shouldn't. My father always said it would get me killed. Little did he know; it was coming close to death so many times that made me crave the danger. There's a sense of invincibility that comes with surviving things that would break most men. Ronan Cole is a destroyer, and I want him to ruin me, but I want to be his mutual destruction. Our little game of power is nothing more than a battle of wills, and I'm not sure if I'm winning or losing.

I don't want to lose...

I push off the bed, go to the bathroom, and turn the shower taps to hot. A small cloud of steam billows over the shower door, and I step under the spray. The hot water feels like lava on my newly branded neck. *I cannot believe he branded me like a breeding cow.* I wash the blood from my body, remaining under the water until the room is full of steam—until I know that any hidden cameras will be completely fogged in mist, then I get out. I dry myself off and slip into the thick robe hanging on the door before I go to the toilet and remove the lid, reaching inside. My fingers brush the edge of the phone placed on the pipe inside, and I take it out, tucking it into the folds of my robe. I quickly cross the bedroom and step onto the balcony. My entire body trembles against the cold as I press a shaking finger against the power button. The screen illuminates and I wait a few seconds. I've checked it every day, waiting for my 'friend' to tell me what they want, to give me a way out. This phone has become a warped form of hope. The screen flashes with a text message. My heart picks up as I read over it: *In the office, there is a painting of the Khimki forest, behind it you will find a safe. The code is 030565. Inside you will find a small black USB drive. Replace it with the one you have. Await further instructions.*

The one I have? I don't have... I turn the phone off, snapping it shut. I tuck it into the folds of my robe again and take it back to the bathroom, placing it back in the tank, propped against the pipe so it doesn't get wet. I rush over to the chest of drawers, grabbing my clutch and glancing inside. *Well, this is some James Bond shit.* There, in the bottom of the bag, is a black USB stick. *How do these people keep putting shit in my bag? How the hell do they know there's a safe, or the code?* This must be Ronan. But then, it's almost so obvious that I don't think it is. Playing childish little games to catch me isn't his style. It's beneath him. Whoever this is, they must have someone in Ronan's house. I can't help but smile at the idea that Ronan, lord of all he surveys, is being fucked over by one of his own. I just know how much that would burn him.

I lie on my bed, thinking through all the ways this could possibly bite me in the ass. Even if I do manage to get into his office and to the safe to swap the sticks...what if I get caught with it? Ronan is going to kill me eventually, so what do I have to lose? The thought should bring a sense of recklessness with it, but it doesn't. I'm not completely without sense, I fear Ronan. I fear his brutality just as much as I crave it, and I wonder, what would he do to me? There are worse fates than death—I'm aware of that—and I have no doubt that Ronan knows every one of them. I keep waiting for the moment when he snaps and unleashes the beast I know lingers just beneath all that refinery. I've pushed him, but none of that would compare to stealing from him, deceiving him. Helping an apparent enemy. But then, aren't I the enemy? His enemy is my friend. This is what I've wanted all along, to take him down from the inside.

I'm going to do it. I'm going to risk everything on the word of a stranger I will likely never meet, all to destroy the man who took my power from me.

It's past eleven when I leave my room, quietly pulling the door closed behind me. I tiptoe down the stairs, and I quickly make my way through the dark house. The occasional hum of voices drifts down the hallway, and I pause outside one of the rooms when I hear Ronan's voice. The door is barely cracked and I peek through. Ronan's sitting on the sofa with his back to the hall, a cloud of smoke sifting through the air. Another man sits in the chair across from him in a three-piece suit looking every bit as rich as Ronan, but lacking the raw power that Ronan seems to physically breathe. There's the distinct low rumble of his laugh. *Good.* Hopefully that will keep him occupied for a minute.

I carry on to his office, my pulse drumming as I try the handle. The door isn't locked and I think that's stupid, but then again, who would be insane enough to break into Ronan Cole's office? Light from the hallway spills into the room, and I catch a glimpse of that painting right behind the desk when I step in and close the door behind me. The room plunges into darkness except for the moonlight shining through the windows. In two corners of the room, those little red lights blink. Of course, there would be cameras in here. I have no choice but to tuck my hair into the collar of my robe and hope they can't make out anything in the dark. If I tamper with those cameras, I'll have Ronan's men up my ass in a heartbeat. There's just enough light coming from the window that I can safely cross the room, stopping in front of the painting. I hook my fingers under the frame, and it swings away from the wall revealing a metal safe. There's a keypad with a blinking green light. With shaking fingers, I type out the code: *030565*. The safe beeps and the door clicks open. I can't believe that worked! Inside are folders, several stacks of Rubles, a phone, and a USB stick. I slip the other USB from my pocket and swap them over before slamming the safe shut. The lock clicks with a beep, and I move the painting back in place.

My chest buzzes, my stomach knots, and I hurry out of the room and down the hall. I'm nearly to the foyer when Ronan steps out of the living room, and almost right into me. My heart leaps in my chest and adrenaline fires through my veins. *Oh, god, he's caught me.* The USB stick in my pocket feels like an atomic bomb ready to wipe me out. I force a smile on my face. "Ronan, I was just looking for you." His eyes study my face and fuck; I swear he can see the lie as clear as day.

I'm so screwed.

Chapter 26

Ronan

"Prisoner" – The Weeknd, Lana Del Ray

My gaze trails over her pretty face, over the slight twitch of her lip. My little Krasivaya is up to something... "Aren't you supposed to be tied up?" I ask.

She glares at me. "Takes more than rope to restrain me, Russian."

"So, you've come to show off your pretend freedom?"

"Of course." She cocks a brow and smiles. "And to steal your brandy." She slips past me into the sitting room where one of the servants is waiting with my brandy and the television remote.

I take the glass from his hand and sit as he turns the television to the late-night news. Camilla pours herself a drink, downs it, and then makes another before coming to sit beside me.

"You do know I only tied you up to annoy you?" I say. "I knew you'd get out, and I must say, I admire your determination." I eye the delicate scratches marring her perfect skin.

"Oh, well, in that case..." Rolling her eyes, she tips her drink back.

I direct my attention to the news. Murders, burglaries, another nuclear blast that rocked the Gobi Desert this week—my phone rings in my pocket and I pull it out. Anastasia's name flashes over the screen. "Yes?" I say.

"How could you?" Anastasia gasps. "After everything I did for you. After everything I have given you, and you've already replaced me?"

"Ana," I say sweetly, "Your husband won't allow it, I'm only trying to mend my broken heart."

"With some cheap whore?"

Camilla places her drink on the end table and cocks a curious brow.

"Ana, please don't do this," I whisper, my eyes locked with Camilla's. "Not now. The only reason I'm not with you is because of Nikoli."

Camilla's hands glide over my chest as she leans in and presses her mouth against my neck. "Aw, so romantic," Camilla says, biting her bottom lip. She throws her leg over my thighs and straddles me. Her fingers trail along the side of my neck. I *should* shove her away from me, but there are many things in life that I've chosen not to do...

"I told you I would leave him," Anastasia says. "I told you I would—"

"You *can't* leave him, Ana," I say. Camilla leans in and

nips my ear. "He won't let you and you know it."

A low sob comes across the line followed by Anastasia mumbling something about love.

I fist Camilla's thick hair, leaning my head back against the sofa as I close my eyes. Her nails dig into my face when she grabs my jaw and presses her lips to mine. The taste of brandy washes over my tongue, and I gently push her away. "Ana, come now... you know she could never compare to you," I say glancing at Camilla. There's a slight flicker in her eyes that gives me such a rise.

She presses her mouth below my ear and her hand against my crotch. "If only that were true."

"I don't believe you, Ronan," Anastasia whispers. "I think I was nothing more than a prize for you to win."

Camilla slides away from me and drops to her knees. This is the most beautiful Camilla has ever looked—on her knees, like she's worshipping me. She reaches for my belt and tugs it open, quickly undoing my slacks.

"Ana, you know that's not true." *Your husband's death is the prize.* Camilla's fingers wrap around my dick, and she swipes her warm tongue across the head. I fight a groan.

"I thought you loved me," Ana cries.

And this is the point where I flip the switch: "Ana, surely you know a man like me is incapable of such a trivial emotion?"

Camilla's eyes lock with mine, a small smile touching her lips just before I watch my cock disappear inside her mouth. I fist her hair, my eyes glued to her as she works me over. Each flick of her tongue, each jerk of her hand threatens to send me over the edge. Camilla Estrada is the type of woman any man would pay money for to have on her knees, because this is power in every sense. I shove my cock down her throat, grinning as Camilla takes it without so much as a gag. "Fuck," I groan, tossing my head against the seat.

"Ronan?" Ana whispers.

My cock slips from Camilla's mouth. She holds her hand out to me. Heat spreads through my chest, and I place the phone in her waiting palm. She presses the phone to her ear, her turquoise eyes holding mine as she strokes over my dick. "Ronan's busy right now, Anastasia." Camilla lightly kisses the head of my cock. "I'm going to have to put your desperation on hold." A smug smile graces her lips. "Unless you want to listen." And then she hangs up before swallowing me back in her throat again.

This is where I should stop her. The conversation is done. This is no longer a game between Camilla and Anastasia, but now one between Camilla and I. Heat courses through my veins like boiling lava and just when I'm about to lose all control, I release her hair and shove her face away. I grab my cock and pump over it until I come with a groan, swearing underneath my breath. Closing my eyes, I take a few deep breaths before I look at her with a grin, because I took that power away from her right at the end.

Camilla wipes the corners of her mouth as she pushes to her feet. She rounds the couch, leans over the back, and places a kiss to my neck. "Never is a man more beautiful than when he's at his weakest." She nips at my throat. "You really are magnificent when you come, Russian," she says before walking from the room.

Round and round we go, dancing within each other's depravity like a man gone mad. I fasten my slacks and drag my hand over my face before reaching for my brandy. *Ding*. I grab my phone, reading over the text: *All the Devil's Dust has been mined*. Clutching the phone in my hand, I swallow. So it seems little kitty's time is almost up, and what a travesty that is. She's such a pretty thing, a defiant thing, such a rare piece of work. It seems so cruel to extinguish the life of such a volatile creation, but in the end, business is business, and I'd be a fool not to acknowledge how dangerous my attraction to her is.

I've worked too hard and too long to let a pretty little thing distract me from my course.

Chapter 27

Camilla

"Heart Shaped Box" – Midnight String Quartet

I haven't seen Ronan since last night. The USB stick is hidden in the back of one of the dresser drawers, and I'm waiting. Waiting for the penny to drop, for Ronan to realize its missing, to come storming in here and kill me for what I've done.

I hurry to the bathroom and take out the phone, checking it for the hundredth time today. The screen lights up, and I wait impatiently for it to load. As soon as the screen blinks to life, I see the message: *Tonight, you will go to Cole's nightclub. Go to the ground floor bathroom. Third stall from the door. Leave the USB in the sanitary bin.* Frowning, I turn the phone off and shove it back inside the toilet tank. How do they know I even have it?

The bedroom door creaks open and I panic, quickly sliding the top of the toilet back into place with a clink. I whirl around to find Igor standing in the bathroom door, scowling at me.

"The boss wants you ready in an hour. There's a dress on the bed." And then he turns and walks away. I go back into the bedroom and glance at the tiny black dress on the bed. Short and tight. Something you would wear to a nightclub...

Ronan's palm rests on the small of my back as we pass the line of people waiting to get into the club. My heart slams against my ribs and a sense of anxiety creeps through me. Whoever my little friend is...they're either imbedded deep in Ronan's organization and wielding a disturbing amount of power... or it is, in fact, Ronan and I'm playing right into his trap, walking to my death. Either way, here I am, in front of the very club they told me I'd be visiting with a USB stick stuffed in my bra.

A few people in line glare in our direction when the bouncer hurries to let us into the warm club. Ronan's men fan around him in a well-practiced formation, each one tense and rigid as though they're prepared to take a bullet for him at any moment.

Ronan leads me through the room littered with black, crystal chandeliers and red velvet chairs. There's a dark sensual feel to this club, and if I didn't already know Ronan owned it, I could have guessed. The dance music pounds through the building, causing the floor to pulse beneath my feet. Even though the music is hard, there's a sexy edge to it, especially when I watch the people on the dancefloor sway and grind against each other.

The USB stick wedged between my breasts feels like it's burning me. I'm convinced that at any moment Ronan will ask me for it, right before he puts a bullet between my eyes. Ronan's men shove people away, clearing a path as though he's royalty as he guides me farther into the club.

I turn into him and bring my lips to his ear. "I need to use the bathroom," I say. My heart skitters.

Sighing impatiently, he jerks his head toward a corridor, then leads me to the restroom. I go to step inside, but he stops me, pushing the door open himself and walking inside. Two girls are at the mirrors. Ronan glares at them and they quickly leave. "Go," he says, waving a hand towards the empty stalls.

"You know I can pee on my own..."

Crossing his arms, he leans against the sink. "The last time I trusted you in a women's room alone, you cut your throat open."

"That's a little overdramatic," I say, walking into the third stall from the left and closing the door. I sit on the closed toilet for a second, my stomach bunching. *Shit.* I don't need to go and if I shove that USB stick into an empty plastic bin, it's going to make a noise... at least, I hope it's empty.

"I have somewhere to be." Ronan says.

"I can't go when you're listening." I huff. "Turn on the hand dryer."

The dryer starts. I quickly pull the USB stick out of my bra and deposit it in the bin. There's the muted thud of it hitting the bottom, but I'm certain Ronan wouldn't have heard that over the dryer. I wait a few seconds before I stand up and flush the toilet. When I open the door, Ronan is standing in the same place, his arms folded over his chest and his eyebrows pulled together in a frown. Those full lips of his press together in annoyance. I can't help but want to kiss them because I do so delight in his bad moods. I wash and dry my hands, then follow him outside, my pulse racing.

I've done my part. Whoever my mysterious friend is—I only hope they truly are a friend. They can't possibly be worse than Ronan. He is, after all, the man who is going to kill me. Others may have tried, but he will succeed, and that makes any revenge I can get so damn sweet.

Once we're back in the main club, Ronan wraps an arm around my waist and pulls me to his side. *Such a showman.* People watch as we pass by, their eyes drifting over the pair of us. One man in a suit stares a little too long. His gaze drags over my exposed thighs, and I watch the raging lust rip through his eyes. I used to love having men fall at my feet, but these days...I prefer something a little more challenging, a little more dangerous. The fact that I've been Ronan's captive for weeks—at his mercy—and yet he hasn't fucked me, well, that hasn't escaped me. I know he wants me, and I'd be lying if I said I didn't want him, too. The man has the restraint of a monk.

He guides me to the end of the hall, through a door, and up a stairwell. Ronan presses a code into a keypad and the door beeps before swinging open into a circular room. The walls are nothing but glass, providing an unobstructed view of the club below. There's a desk, a few chairs, and a small bar in the room. Nothing else. Ronan's men follow us in and close the door behind them. As soon as the door closes the room plunges into near silence. I can feel the rhythmic *thump, thump, thump* of the music, but can hear nothing.

Ronan takes a seat at the desk, then points to a chair across from him. "Sit," he instructs.

I do as told, and his men take up positions around the room, placing their backs to the glass. No one says anything, and my nerves are on edge. Just when I'm about to ask what we're waiting for, the door opens, music pours in. Three men walk inside, two in suits, the other is wearing a hoody and ripped jeans. The door slams shut, bringing with it that deafening silence, and the man in the hoody jumps. His gaze shifts anxiously around the room. Sweat beads on his brow as he drags a trembling hand through his messy, blond hair. The suits stop on either side of him, right in front of Ronan's desk. I can practically feel the fear pouring from him, and I almost feel sorry. He looks so young, so completely out of place here in the devil's domain.

Ronan drums his fingers over the desk before lighting a cigar, puffing away as he stares the poor guy down. "I'm very disappointed," he says. "Very, *very* disappointed." *That's so not good for him.*

"Mr. Cole. I don't..." the man chokes out with an American accent. "What did I, I'm sorry, I just—why am I here?"

"Do not speak to me directly again," Ronan says, his jaw ticking.

"Please," he whispers before breaking into tears. The guilty ones always break so fast. I have to wonder what this man could possibly have done to Ronan.

"Igor," Ronan snaps his fingers. "Tell this man what he did."

"Yes, boss." Igor says, stepping from the shadows. He moves in front of the man, standing like a soldier at attention. "You were required to complete a job for Mr. Cole, and paid well for your services. You betrayed him. Traitors are not tolerated."

"They made me. I'd have been arrested for treason!" He cries. "I'm sorry! I will do anything, just, please let me—"

"How cute." Ronan laughs before taking another drag from his cigar.

"Please, don't hurt me!" The man cries and pleads. Like a cornered, wounded deer, he knows the end is nigh. He is not dealing with any predator. This is Ronan Cole. He will find no mercy here.

"Igor, tell him that I own the FBI." Ronan laughs again, and a thick cloud of smoke billows into the air. "And do tell Mr. Thomas that I am not a man of mercy."

All I can hear are the man's hysterical sobs. I huff out a breath and roll my eyes. *Can no one die well anymore?* Igor and the other men disappear through the door, and I catch Ronan glance at me from the corner of my eye. "Come here, little kitty." He scoots his chair away from the desk and pats his thigh.

I push to my feet and walk over to him, a small smile plastered across my lips even as suspicion crawls through me. I never quite trust Ronan, but especially not when he's inviting me so close. I sit on his lap, cross one leg over the other, and drape my arm around his shoulder.

"You seem annoyed." He smirks.

"A traitor should at least have the decency to die well, don't you think?" The man's high-pitched squeals fill the room.

"Of course I do. However, Mr. Thomas here, I mean, look at him." Ronan points across the room. "So unkempt, he doesn't even take pride in his appearance. What makes you think he would take pride in his death?"

I brush my finger over the crisp collar of Ronan's shirt. "What do you expect? He's a traitor." I curl my lip. "To the fucking FBI of all people." *God, I hate the American authorities.*

"He's worked with terrorist organizations in the Middle East. Done deplorable things. Hacking missile codes and aiding in the death of innocent people...children..." Ronan glances at him and tsks. "He showed such promise as a hacker. Tis a shame."

I glance over my shoulder at the man now on his knees with his chin to his chest. "For him, yes." I turn back to Ronan, watching the way his eyes swirl with excitement.

Ronan can be an arrogant asshole, he can be selfish and narcissistic, but this right here is when he's at his most intoxicating. This ruthlessness matches my own, and it makes me want him in the most twisted of ways. My heart pounds. My pussy clenches, and I shift on his lap, trying to focus.

"Just think," Ronan says, resting his cigar on an ashtray. "Had you simply done as told, you could have been solely responsible for putting the next President of the United States into power. You would have been two-million dollars richer, but you allowed your selfishness to cloud your judgement and now..." Ronan shrugs. "You'll just die a dirty little traitor."

"Please! I can pay you..." the man says.

"Pay *me*?" Ronan laughs hysterically.

"Jesus fuck." I snap. "Does he look like he needs money to you?" *Stupid shit.* Ronan's hand lands on my thigh.

"Tell me, what would you do to him, Camilla?" Ronan whispers, sweeping his finger along my jaw. My pulse thrums hard beneath his touch.

"My father once told me a traitor's death should be beautiful, memorable." Ronan's fingers grip my thigh harder and he grins.

"All death is beautiful."

I trail my nails over the seam of his collar where it meets his skin. "Nothing is more beautiful than blood, such a vibrant color." I tilt my head. "So pretty." His hand leisurely moves over my hip, shifting me closer.

"So festive," he breathes against my lips, and for a moment I allow myself to get lost in the tension crackling between us. "How would you kill him? Tell me, Camilla." His fingers draw circles on my skin.

I shrug one shoulder. "Take a knife," I trace my fingers over Ronan's jaw and up to his temple. "Start here, and cut." My fingers drift down to his chin. "And then, I'd dig my fingernails underneath the loose skin and slowly peel it away from his face." He grins, and I lean in, brushing my lips over his neck before I bite his earlobe. "But the real secret is, if you burn the exposed muscle they don't bleed out as fast." I force myself to pull back, because I'm so turned on right now.

One of Ronan's brows twitches before his smile deepens. "You are so savage," he says. I can feel his cock swelling underneath my ass. "Tell me, is there much blood?" Another noticeable swell of his cock. He gets off on this shit, on the brutality and the violence, on the poetry of taking a man's life.

"Of course. If you really want a party, you can always cut out the eyes." I can't tear my gaze from Ronan. I'm drunk on him, on us.

He leans next to my ear. "This is what makes me want to fuck you, little kitty."

"Then fuck me," I breathe, raking my fingers into his hair as I tilt my head to the side. His teeth sink into my neck. His grip on my hips tightens and he hisses out a breath as I squirm on his lap.

The door opens, and I snap out of whatever daze Ronan has me in. The rapid breaths and desperate sobs from the man whose life is near its end return. Igor steps into the room, the noise from the club returning for only a moment before it's silenced again. Igor mumbles something in Russian to the other two men. They nod and cross the room, coming back with a harness which they lay out on the floor. Ronan pushes me to my feet before he stands and walks to the side of the room, humming. He fiddles with something on the bar, and the eerie sound of a lone cello comes crackling through hidden speakers. On his way back to his desk, Ronan moves his finger through the air like a conductor at a symphony. Power may be what he enjoys, but this is what he craves. A monster in his cave, the angel of death at a funeral.

Ronan grabs his cigar, once again puffing away as he stares at poor Mr. Thomas. The haunting notes wind around me as they crawl through the room. I sit on the edge of his desk as he comes to stand next to me.

"Is this...Nirvana?" I ask. Nirvana on the cello. Only Ronan.

"But of course." He grins. "Heart Shaped Box."

"Of course."

His hand clasps the back of my neck, his eyes wild. "I do love the irony of it. The refined edge it brings to such a brutal act."

The men approach Mr. Thomas, and he fights his captors tooth and nail, as any animal fighting for survival would. Finally, after several punches to the face and gut, he's in the harness. Igor presses a button on a remote and a low whirring sound fills the room as the guy is slowly lifted by his legs into the air, suspended from a winch in the ceiling. He pleads and begs and cries, but surely he can see we're well past that? Beyond the glass windows people drink and dance in the club below. They revel in the simplicity of life while inside these walls, death rules supreme in the form of Ronan Cole. The king sitting on his throne. Lord of all he surveys. Nothing outside of this room is of consequence to him. We are removed from the meagre troubles of everyone else.

Igor steps up to Mr. Thomas and I catch the light glint from a blade. "Igor," Ronan says, "Wait." Igor halts. "Would you like to have the honors?" Ronan focuses his attention on me as he strokes my hair behind my ear.

I smile. "And I thought you were mean." To take a person's life...well it's an addiction that can never truly be cured once tasted. There's nothing like the rush that comes with watching a man's very essence leave his eyes. It's powerful, hypnotic, utterly exhilarating; just like Ronan himself.

Ronan holds out his palm and motions Igor over. Worry flashes across Igor's face as he places the knife into Ronan's grip. "Leave," Ronan says, and without a word, all the men vanish from the room. The lock to the door clicks, and Ronan moves between my thighs.

I hold out my hand, and he places the knife on my palm. "Just his face, or the eyes as well?" The sound of the music blends with Mr. Thomas' cries creating a beautifully haunting crescendo.

"Let me teach you how to make this into an art." Ronan's eyes gleam. "Fine art is always refined." He slowly trails his finger across my throat. "One simple slice, and all the blood will drain from his body. So slow. So perfect." He grabs my chin and stares down at me. "Killing this way is what separates us from the animals."

"Well," I smirk, "we can't taint that distinguished image of yours now, can we?" I nip his bottom lip before I hop off the desk, walking slowly over to the man hanging upside down from the ceiling.

"Please! Please! Please! Please!" he says over and over, his words slurred and frantic.

"Shhh." I drop to a crouch in front of him and twist my head to the side to look at him. "Shhhh. It's okay." I press my fingers to his lips and he quiets, tears cascading over his temples. "You won't feel a thing." I grin and prick the blade into the side of his neck. He whimpers, and a drop of blood wells in the gash. I catch it and swipe my finger over his lips, coating them with his own blood as I draw a smile on his face. "Smile, you do get to keep your face." He chokes, and I slide the blade across his throat in one slow sweep. He screams and thrashes as a fountain of blood pours over his face. The gurgle of him drowning in his own blood sends a jolt of adrenaline down my spine before I stand and turn to face Ronan.

His eyes lock on me as he stalks toward me. He stops in front of me, hesitating for a second before he snatches the knife. My heart skitters and skips, because I have no idea what he's about to do. Without warning, he grabs my shoulders and slams me against the glass wall, the tip of the blade pricking underneath my chin as he leans in. "How would you kill me today, Krasivaya?"

My breath catches. "Have you heard of death by a thousand cuts?" I swallow. "I'd cut you all over, and then maybe I'd fuck you while you bled for me." There's the constant drip of Mr. Thomas' blood splattering the floor beside me.

"Would you?" he whispers against my lips. "I want to cut you so badly."

"Hmm." I scratch my nails over the back of his neck. "There's nothing quite like the feel of slick blood on hot skin."

His forehead touches mine and he inhales on a groan as the blade of the knife sweeps over my jaw. I tremble, and an unsteady breath leaves my lips. "I bet you're so pretty when you *really* bleed."

"So..." I lean in, bringing my lips to his ear, "make me bleed." Adrenaline fires through my veins until I'm high on the danger, the thrill, brimming with lust and need for the man in front of me. He's my adversary and my reflection and I want him. Just once.

His eyes churn with sadistic urges, and he bites at his lip. The cool tip of the blade slides down to my collarbone. I watch his nostrils flare, his eyes focus, and then a searing pain floods my body as he slowly slices across my chest. Swallowing, he stares at the cut before leaning down and licking over the fresh wound, and I close my eyes on a moan.

"I should kill you," he whispers.

"You should."

He raises the knife to my throat and holds it there. His gaze keeps drifting to the cut on my chest, the sight, I think, gnawing away at restraint. Closing his eyes, he fists my hair as though to steady himself. The sharp edge of the blade pierces my skin again, and my heart pounds furiously. This is it. He's going to kill me, but what a beautiful way to go...

The prick of the blade disappears. Ronan groans,

dropping the knife before he grabs me and slams me to the floor. He swipes one hand through my blood, and rips my underwear off with the other. My legs fall shamelessly open for him, and he pinches my swollen clit between his fingers.

"You're bleeding for me, little kitty, but I want you to beg for me."

I fist his hair, pulling hard at the roots. "I don't beg, Russian."

A deep laugh rumbles up his throat as he yanks his belt open and reaches for the knife on the floor. The blade glints in the light as he brings it back to my throat. My heart slams against my ribs, my lungs struggle for air, and the rush of adrenaline makes me almost blind with need.

The music, the sound of a man dying next to me, the scent of blood in the air, the people on the other side of that glass so blissfully unaware... and Ronan, it's a heady combination that I don't have the will to fight. I want him. I want this, the depravity, the lust, the anger and the hate. His hand lands on my throat and the knife presses under my chin. He squeezes just hard enough to threaten my oxygen intake and make my vision dot. I can feel how close he is, riding that razor-sharp edge of control. He's every bit as mindless as I am, and I want him to fall with me.

He drops the knife again and grips the inside of my thigh as his body presses over mine, hard and heavy. Our eyes lock, and I see the promise of blood and pain. I'm not sure if he wants to fuck me or kill me. Perhaps both. Smiling,

I spread my legs wider, an invitation. He growls before slamming inside me so brutally hard that it takes my breath away. Within a single moment, he consumes me and decimates me, and I know I will never be the same again. His tongue trails along my neck. "If only I could watch you bleed like that," he whispers, nodding toward the man hanging from the ceiling, gurgling through his last dying breaths.

I slam my lips against his, biting until the metallic taste of his blood fills my mouth. He groans, and I wrap my legs around him, forcing him deeper. So fucking deep—until I don't know where he ends and I begin. It's all one bloody, perilous mess. An endless pool of destruction that is sure to ruin us both. On a moan, I throw my head against the floor, and he fucks me harder, faster. His nails bite into my neck, a sweet threat and a deadly promise. My vision swims. My pulse throbs desperately. The room whirls around me as he tries to fuck himself into me. He's trying to claim ownership of my soul, and I'm not sure if he's going to kill me to take it. I love it. But I want it. I've never been so close to the ragged edge of pleasure and pain—life and death. I'm being possessed by the devil and he can have me. His tongue brushes mine and his grip on my neck flexes.

"You are so pretty when you bleed," he mumbles against my lips before shoving my face away. He shifts, and I feel the sharp prick of the knife at the base of my throat before he drags it down my chest, slicing my skin. Pain and pleasure blend together in perfect chemistry. My pussy clamps around him as an orgasm tears through me so hard and fast I'm not sure if my heart physically stops beating.

His movements grow frantic and he drops the knife to the floor, wrapping both hands around my throat. "You are beautiful, Camilla. So fucking perfect." His hold becomes painful. He growls, thrusting into me so hard and fast that my mind jumbles, my lungs scream for oxygen and then everything goes black.

When I wake up, I'm lying in the same spot, my body aching in the most beautiful way. I sit up and glance at the body lightly swinging from the ceiling. The scent of blood and cigar smoke fill my senses and the floor vibrates to the low beat of club music pulsing beneath us. Blood slowly slides across the wooden floor, circling a small drain, and Ronan's across the room, watching it. I push to my feet and skirt around the drain as I make my way toward Ronan. His eyes slowly roam over my body, stopping on my throat.

"You had a drain put in your office?" I say, my voice still hoarse from the brutal grip he held on my windpipe.

"Some men want plasma screens; I simply want a drain." He grins.

I push between his thighs and place a hand on his chest. "And a winch in the ceiling." I lift a brow. "Anyone would think you like to get your hands dirty, Russian."

He loosens his tie before slipping it over his head and placing the soft fabric against my chest. His eyes remain trained on the cuts while he wipes the blood from my skin. "My hands *are* clean, little kitty."

"Uh-huh." I glance pointedly at his blood covered tie.

Ronan slips his jacket back on and adjusts his collar. He combs through my hair, using it to cover the cuts on my shoulder and chest. "Come on."

He leads me across the room, and the second the door opens, the sound from the club surrounds me. One of the men waiting outside slips into the room and closes the door behind him, I guess to clean up the mess. Just like that, everything that happened feels like a deep dark secret that only those walls will ever know.

Ronan's hand grips my hip as we move down the stairs and through the club. He stops at the edge of the bar to speak to someone. People dance around me, laughing and grinding against each other. When I look over at Ronan, he's moved to a side door, going over paperwork with another man in a suit. Someone bumps into my side and I snap my head around to glare at them. My gaze collides with a broad chest, and I lift my eyes to the man now staring down at me with a lascivious smile. He says something in Russian as his hand lands on my waist, pulling me tight against his body and forcing me backwards across the bar. I snarl and shove against him until I feel a wall at my back. His hand goes to my thigh, pushing my dress up. I can't move. He's heavy, and pressed so tightly against me I can't even lift my arm, or knee him in the balls. His hand drifts higher and I panic.

He growls something in my ear. I don't have to be able to speak Russian to know his intentions. *How the fuck did I end up in this position?*

Suddenly, he stiffens. His eyes widen, his body goes rigid tense, and he groans. There's a snap as his head twists violently to the side, then he hits the floor. Ronan's right in front of me like an avenging angel. My gaze drifts from Ronan to the guy at my feet—dead—his neck snapped.

He smooths a hand down the front of his jacket and holds out his hand to me. People around us panic and scatter, but Ronan is all I see. Taking his hand, I step over the body. I can feel the rage radiating from him, see the blood lust and death dancing in his eyes like the very flames of hell. I always want Ronan to lose control, but right now, as I look at him, I'm not sure I want to see this beast out of his cage. And I know he's rattling the bars, because Ronan just got his hands dirty. For me. To protect me. No one has ever protected me. *Shit.*

Chapter 28

Ronan

"Eye" – Smashing Pumpkins

Adrenaline jolts through me like a live wire as I usher Camilla through the club. My pulse throbs in my jugular and I clench my jaw, fighting back the urge I have to slam my fist through a wall. I just snapped a man's neck simply because he touched her. I lost control, but my god, it seems the pits of hell have opened up to offer me this woman...

I push the exit door open and step into a flurry of snow. The waiting car pulls toward the exit as I walk down the steps, Camilla following behind me. The car stops and the driver nods as he hurries around to open the door for us. Once inside, I take a breath and stare at her. Neither of us know what just happened, who won or who lost, and that's not a situation I like to be in.

"I had that under control," Camilla says, breaking the silence.

I swallow, attempting to calm my racing pulse. "You never know when to shut the fuck up, do you?" My teeth grind together, red flashes before my eyes. She glares at me, and I grab her by the throat before placing my face directly in front of hers. "Do not think for one second that you mean anything to me. Me fucking you means nothing." Her pulse thrums beneath my fingertips, calling to the monster inside.

"Good." Her breath caresses my lips. "Then remember, I'm not a fucking damsel, and you're no prince."

"No, you aren't a damsel, because in the stories the damsel is always saved, isn't she?" I smirk. "And you will never be saved, little kitty, because I'm the man who will end your life."

She groans. "God, you're such a dick." She grabs the front of my jacket and slams her lips against mine, her tongue thrusting inside my mouth.

My hold on her throat tightens. I shove away from her, my grip growing stronger by the second. I close my eyes and all I can see is the image of her covered in her own blood, the way her eyes danced when she was handed the blade to slit that man's throat. My eyes flash open.

"You could just end it right now." She dares. "Just squeeze a little tighter, Russian."

A surge of adrenaline courses through me, and I squeeze just a little harder. All she does is close her eyes and smile. I watch her fight it. I watch her beautiful skin pit around my fingertips, and that fine line of control I cling to snaps like a frayed string. I strangle her until she chokes for a breath, and then I slowly inch my face toward hers. "Is that tight enough?" I whisper against her lips.

She chokes again and I can't help but kiss her. Hard. She meets me blow for blow, tongue and teeth and rage. The way she unhinges me— I want to kill her for it just as much as I need to fuck her, and I find my grip loosening. She moves and straddles my thighs, pushing up on her knees and forcing my head back over the seat. Her teeth sink into my bottom lip before she breaks away, pressing her forehead against mine. Clinging to the last semblance of control, I move my hands to her waist, gripping them as though she may keep me rooted.

"Thank you," she whispers, placing a trembling hand on my jaw before she kisses me again. The rage and hate retreat like a rising wave melting back into the ocean. The warmth of her lips sends a calming flood through my veins, and even though I hate that she has this control over me, I relish in it. The warmth of her body, the scent of blood in her hair—it's nearly too much. Suddenly, she breaks away, staring at me as her brows pull together in a frown. And then, she climbs off me, putting as much space as possible between us.

When we arrive home, she walks straight into the house, disappearing down the hallway without a word. *She's lost inside her own mind, much like myself,* I think as I retire to my office.

The fire roars in the fire place, the kindling popping and crackling under the heat. Dragging a hand down my face, I fall back in the chair. I watch the red flames lick over the logs, thinking, questioning. Tides shift often in life, I'm just not certain whether I like the new direction I'm being taken.

My phone buzzes in my pocket. I glance at Anastasia's name flashing over the screen when I pull it out. "What do you want?" I ask, my gaze still fixated on the fire that reminds me so much of my little kitty.

"Ronan." She's crying. "I love you. Please, *please...*"

"I don't have time for this any longer, Anastasia. Don't call me again."

I disconnect the call and immediately block her number before I place the phone on my lap. Soon enough my plan will be tied into a nice, neat bow, and maybe then my head will clear.

The setting sun spills through the stained-glass window, casting a kaleidoscope of colors over the Ruger on my desk. I haven't seen Camilla since last night, since I watched her slit a man's throat and fucked her in her own blood...

A video call dings on my phone and I accept it, waiting as the blurry image of Kristoff's face comes into focus. Behind him the Mexican landscape spreads out like a canvas, the sun high over the now empty lake.

"What do you want me to do with the Mexican?" he asks.

"Just let him be."

His brow furrows. "You have no use for him now? No?"

"No, but he'll eventually get himself killed off in one of his petty little cartel wars. Thank you for overseeing the project, Kristoff."

"Of course." He smiles, and I disconnect the call.

I have absolutely no use for Gabriel Estrada or the Juarez cartel now, but he does not know that, and he never needs to. Glancing through the open doorway, I watch Camilla leisurely stroll into the living room and grab the decanter of brandy. I could very easily keep playing this game. Continue to have the cartels smuggle ammunition into America. I'm sure, to them, it would be a legitimate enough reason for me to hold Camilla. They, of course, have no idea what my plans truly are, so I could keep her if I wanted.

And I do want to, but therein lies the problem. I should not *want* to keep her. She will constantly fight me and hate me, and it's just a distraction, a form of amusement that could cost me gravely. Camilla is too unhinged—much like I was before I learned to control that monster lurking inside. Too unhinged, yet she is too magnificent to blot from existence.

Stop it! I slam my fist over the desk before I drag my hand down my face. Lust is powerful, I am well aware of this, and that woman strips me to nothing but animalistic urges. She makes me want to hurt her, fuck her, own her. I snapped a man's neck simply because he touched what I deem as mine, and a man such as I cannot afford an emotion that inflicts such rash decisions. Closing my eyes, I remember how she let me cut her and fuck her, how beautifully twisted her mind is. God, she is ruthless. *A queen fit for a king...* But not every king needs a queen.

My gaze drifts back through the doorway to Camilla. I don't need a queen, but goddam it, I want that one, because there is no other woman who could stand a chance at holding equal power. But I could never trust her... My mind is doing numbers on me. I'm on a pendulum, swinging back and forth between my desire to kill her and my will to keep her. I watch her move around the den, my cock swelling with each passing second. My gaze drifts back to the gun. I could let fate decide. Empty a few bullets and pull the trigger once. A heads or tails toss of the coin, except with a gun...

The intercom crackles and a guard's panicked voice shouts through the speakers. "Anastasia is here!"

"Send her away," I say shoving the gun into the drawer.

"She rammed through the gate, sir. She's already at the door. We thought of shooting her, bu—"

"Shooting her? Since when has having the President's wife shot on my property sounded like a good idea?" I push up from the desk. "I'll handle this."

Groaning, I roll my eyes and head into the foyer just before someone pounds angrily over the door. I sigh, shaking my head as I yank the door open. Anastasia comes barreling inside, her blonde hair in disarray, mascara smudge below her eyes, and I can just make out the fine mist of blood across her pale cheeks. *Wonderful. Derevichi must be dead.*

"You have to help me," she says before breaking down into sobs and falling dramatically to the floor. I roll my eyes again and shake my head.

"You shouldn't be here, Ana."

"I killed him! For you!" she shouts as she pushes to her feet. "I killed him for you, Ronan, because I love you. We can be together." She paces the foyer, combing her hands through her hair. She stops by the doorway and stares at me with wild eyes. “We can be together!” This is what the weakness of love does to people, it drives them mad. It takes away their control. I can't help but smirk at the thought.

The tap of heels over the marble echoes into the ceiling. Ana glances behind me and glares. I spin around as Camilla crosses the room, her dark hair swaying with each seductive swish of her hips.

"Ana," I say, still staring at Camilla, "leave."

When I turn to look at Anastasia she's still glaring at Camilla, her chest rising in ragged swells. "Ana, do not—" I go to step toward her, and that's when I notice the bloodied blade clasped tightly in her hand.

On a growl, Anastasia throws herself at Camilla, wildly swinging the knife. Camilla doesn't flinch or move, simply back hands Ana across the face with such force that her head snaps to the side. Effortlessly, Camilla snatches the knife before fisting her hair and yanking her head back.

"I fucking warned you," Camilla says, slashing the blade over Anastasia's throat. Beautiful ruby blood spills from the gash and Ana's eyes go wide as she chokes. Camilla smiles and pulls Ana close, the blood drenching her.

Several of my men storm into the room and I hold up a hand. "Leave," I say to them. Camilla brushes a piece of Anastasia's hair behind her ear, whispers something in Spanish that I can't quite make out, and then she lets go of her. Ana's body crumples to the floor in a pool of blood. My pulse races, my skin catches fire first with lust, then with rage.

The freshly murdered President's wife lays slain in the middle of my foyer. Within a matter of seconds, Camilla has ruined my perfectly orchestrated plan, creating a mess for me to clean up. Flashes of red dance in my vision. My chest grows tight with fury. "Camilla," I manage to say calmly as I step over Anastasia's body. "Come with me."

Tis a shame to slaughter such a pretty little thing, but to all things there must come an end.

Chapter 29

Camilla

"Bury Me Facedown" – Grandson

Ronan's fingers dig into my arm as he drags me to his office. I can literally hear his uneven breaths when he shoves me inside. The door locks behind me, and I clutch the knife in my hand so hard that my knuckles throb. A vein in his temple pops and thumps, his lips lay flat on his face, and his eyes... they're flaming like the inner circle of hell. I've never seen Ronan so mad, not when I've pushed him, not when he killed that man in the club last night. He's practically boiling over with it.

"What was I supposed to do?" I ask, already plotting how I can rationalize with him on this.

His eyes flutter shut. "Years." He takes a breath and his jaw tics. "I fucked that woman for *years* for this *very* night, and you ruined it all because of your lack of control!" he shouts, his voice booming into the rafters. "And now, *now* I have to formulate an entire new plan to get rid of her fucking body, fake her disappearance." He drags a hand through his hair. "All while I am trying to ensure the American election goes accordingly." He shakes his head. "Can no one do anything right?"

"Fine. I'm sorry, but I'm sure your world domination will ensue." The mad rage in his eyes makes me take a step back.

"You do not understand the art." He storms toward me. “The beauty in the way something is executed. It was planned perfectly and you just shit all over it!" I take several steps away from him and grip the knife harder, pressing it into the folds of my dress. He's going to kill me. I've always been prepared for this eventuality, unafraid even, but when faced with the reality of your death...well, survival instincts scream awfully loud. "You are stupid," he grabs my chin, squeezing hard. "And defiant. And not worth the air that you breathe."

"Fuck you, Russian," I snarl and swing the knife at his neck. The blade meets the side of his throat and he ducks away, but not before the satisfying sight of blood greets me.

His hand goes to his throat. When he pulls it away, he stares down at his bloodied palm, and then a smile reminiscent of the Cheshire cat slowly inches across his lips. "You made me bleed," he says, pleasure dancing in his tone. "How exciting!" That wild look in his eyes makes me nervous and, for the first time in my life, I truly feel like cornered prey.

I take another unsteady step back, eyeing the door and

Ronan's position. He smiles like the devil, his white collar quickly turning crimson as blood runs down his neck. "What a shame, I missed the artery," I say, my voice shaky even to my own ears. My flight instinct finally overrides everything else, and I dart around him, slashing the knife in his direction. I scream when he catches me by the hair. My head snaps back and burning pain rips over my scalp. He yanks me toward him and my chest hits my back. His other hand grips my wrist squeezing so hard that my fingers flex and the knife clatters to the floor. "Are you going to kill me, Russian?" I laugh.

"*God* yes," he says with a deep groan.

I struggle in his hold, my heart pounding in my chest. "Then do it!" I struggle to turn my face toward him, the blood from his neck smearing across my cheek. The pain shooting through my scalp suddenly subsides, and then I feel a single finger swipe across my cheek. I watch his bloodied finger lift away, then hear him suck it into his mouth.

"So good," he moans. And without warning, he spins me around and shoves me facedown onto his desk. "I'll give you everything you want, Camilla. Me and death all at the same time." He slams a palm over the side of my face, crushing my cheek against the hard wood. My heart beats in a desperate pleading rhythm, demanding that I run, that I survive, but like the sick addict I've become, I crave him, even at his worst. *Especially* at his worst. If Ronan Cole is going to kill me then I want to buy a favor with the devil one more time before I die. I reach back and slowly inch the hem of my dress up my thighs and over my ass. A low chuckle rumbles from his throat. "What a compliment. I'm going to kill you, and you still want to fuck me..."

"Don't pretend it doesn't turn you on, the violence of it all." I grin. "The blood."

"Oh," he drags his hand down to my throat, one by one wrapping his fingers around it before he presses his cock against me. "You have *no* idea."

My mind freefalls down this morbid little rabbit hole Ronan has dragged me to. Down, down, down I go until all I want is him, to dance with the devil, to corrupt my soul so entirely that only he could possibly want it. "Then fuck me, one last time. And make it good."

From the corner of my eye, I can barely catch him swipe his finger through the blood on his throat, and then he rubs it over my lips and up my cheek. "Such a shame," he says before I hear the clink of his belt buckle, "I almost thought I'd met my match." And with that, he slams into me so hard and deep that I gasp. My nails claw over the wood of the desk. He grabs my wrists and pins them together at the small of my back, forcing my back to bow. He slides impossibly deep, forcing a sharp bite of pain as he jerks my head back. My spine aches as he thrusts into me. It's cruel and brutal in the most blissful way.

"We could have made such a perfect pair," he says,

leaning over me and slamming his mouth against mine.

"We'd burn everything around us to the ground." We would. We'd be like a spark in a world built of tinder wood. We'd destroy everything.

"Sit on thrones of skulls and bones..." He bites my lip. Hard. The bitter taste of blood fills my mouth. "But I could never trust you, and you could never trust me."

He thrusts harder, making me moan. "I'd kill you," I gasp.

"That's a lie." He buries himself inside me, holding himself there. He releases my wrists and wraps his hand around my throat and pulls me up, bringing my chest away from the desk. "You crave this," he whispers against my ear. *God, I do. So much.*

I turn my head, nipping at his jaw. "We often crave that which kills us."

His hot breaths fan across my neck; his hand tightens around my throat. He fucks me like he's trying to kill me and save me at the same time. Like I'm worthless, yet irrevocably precious. I know I'm going to die. I can feel it in every thrust, every threatening squeeze of his fingers, every whispered kiss over my neck. This is the end of our bloodstained road. The final battle.

Without warning, he pulls out of me, flipping me over on the desk and pulling me up. I wrap my legs around his hips and he slides back inside of me, slow. Steady. His eyes lock with mine. "Tell me how I should kill you." He kisses my lips softly. "How do you want to die?" His tongue swipes up the side of my neck and he bites my shoulder. It's brutal and raw and soul shattering.

"What if I don't want to die?" I rake my fingers into his hair and tug his head to the side, tracing my tongue over his bloodied neck. A low growl rumbles through him as I moan.

"Mm," he mumbles before kissing me again, his tongue slipping between my lips. "I promise I'll make it pretty. I just want you to bleed for me, Camilla."

I can picture Ronan slitting my throat, watching me bleed with that wild, unhinged lust in his eyes. I want it. I want to make him utterly lose control just once before I die. "Then cut me," I whisper in his ear. "Fuck me while I bleed for you. Come inside me while you watch me die." Groaning, he slams into me on a hard thrust. His weight shifts and reaches for something on the desk behind me. When he moves back, he holds the letter opener up.

“You want to bleed?” he says, fucking me.

My heart skips a beat, and a sick smile pulls at his lips. I focus on him as he raises it and slams it into my thigh. Blinding pain rips through me, causing my head to spin. I bite the inside of my cheek on a scream and glance down at the metal handle sticking out of my leg. Blood wells around it before running down either side of my thigh.

"You wouldn't even scream for me.” He sighs. “Such a shame." With a sadistic grin, he grabs the handle and yanks it out, then brings it to his mouth, slipping the dull blade between his lips. "I have something else in mind for you, little kitty." He tosses the letter opener to the side. "Although, I do love to watch you bleed."

His mouth covers mine as he thrusts into me hard. The taste of my blood coats his tongue, and god, it's arousing. He fucks me like he's possessed. The pain lances up my leg, blending with the torturous pleasure he's coaxing from me, the simple knowledge that death is so near. I throw my head back and he bites my neck, and I come for him, screaming his name like it's a sacrificial offering and I am at his altar. I have nothing more to give because he has taken everything.

Growling into my neck, he grabs my hips and slams deep inside me, stilling. He stays there, his hot, ragged breaths washing over my neck before his lips brush my throat. "Don't move," he whispers. There's a storm swirling through his eyes, a look of anticipation—the same look that possessed him right before I slit that man's throat. "Don't." He hesitates, his mouth hovering over mine. "Move." My body shakes from the adrenaline and bliss running rampant through my veins. This is fear, I suppose, and as much as I hate it, it makes me feel alive.

Ronan rounds the desk, slowly, methodically, his eyes trained on me like the prey that I am. A smile plays over his lips when he opens the drawer. I glance at the revolver now in his hand, almost disappointed that he hasn't planned something more violent. He stops in front of me, making a show of emptying three bullets before slamming the cylinder back into place and spinning it. "I kill you now, I watch you bleed for a moment, but..." A deep grin sets on his face. "I keep you, and I can watch you bleed time and time again. Such a dilemma."

He leans over me, pressing my body into the hard wood of the desk. His finger strokes over my cheek and a trembling breath leaves my lips. I'm practically shaking with anticipation and fear. I want to hate him. I want to loathe him for everything that he is and everything that he's done but I can't, because I understand power, and this is what it is to wield it. The very thing that may kill me is the thing I crave so relentlessly, because Ronan is the embodiment of the power he possesses. I'm a threat to his control, to that power, he just has no idea how much. I beam as I think of some unknown enemy of his holding whatever information is on that USB drive.

I crave Ronan. He craves me. I want to kill him, and he's going to kill me. But I will win in the end because I took something from him and he doesn't even know.

Rage and destruction runs rampant through his eyes when he nudges the cold barrel of the gun beneath my chin. I stare at him. I can barely breathe, barely think through the rush of panic that assaults me. My heart thumps in my throat and tears prick my eyes against my will. I don't want to die, but I refuse to die badly. I've watched too many men refuse to accept their fate, knowing they've wronged me, knowing the price for such an act. I haven't wronged Ronan, but from the day I was old enough to understand my place in my father's empire I have accepted that I will die like this eventually. Honestly, it could have been worse. A bullet is a kindness in my world. Tears spill over my temples traitorously and Ronan tilts his head.

"Ah, there it is." He inhales, smiling. "Finally, I've found your fear."

"I'm not afraid," I whisper.

He sweeps a hand down my face, wiping away my tears. "You don't have to lie to me, I find it beautiful, Camilla. Everyone has a weakness. It's what makes us human."

"Then I suppose you are mine, Ronan Cole."

Closing his eyes, he sighs as the grin on his face deepens. "I *know* I am." The gun presses harder underneath my chin and I gasp. "Three bullets, six cylinders," he says, his lips brushing mine. "And one click decides your fate. I *almost* hope you survive."

I close my eyes, picturing the moment that bullet tears through my skull, the blood and brain matter coating Ronan's face—the taste of death on his lips.

"One," he breathes, kissing me reverently. My heart pounds so fast it's all I can hear, my own morbid symphony. "Two." Another soft kiss, and he smiles against my lips. "Three..."

THE END

Please don't stab us. <3

Printed in Great Britain
by Amazon

64934212R00147